IMPERIAL PUBLISHING HOUSE
PRESENTS

SLIM AND
THE LADY

BY TONYA

Tonya

ISBN: 978-1-943179-51-0

Published by Imperial Publishing House a subsidiary of Nayberry Publications
www.imperialpublishinghouse.com

Chapter 1

Last night's hangover was still evident. His eyes were bloodshot. His lips were crusty and white. *A shower would fix it,* he thought. He moved as quickly as his pounding headache would let him. Then, he showered and dressed for work.

"I got to stop drinking," he said as he looked at his haggard reflection in the mirror. It'd been over a year, and it was time to move on.

On his way to work, he stopped by McDonald's for coffee and a biscuit. He still made it to work with time to spare. As soon as he got into the building, he knew something was wrong. People were speaking in harsh tones and rushing about. There were shocked expressions and dazed people wandering aimlessly.

Downsizing was the word they used. He, along with about three hundred other people in his department, was let go. Slim had expected something like this to happen, so he was prepared. He'd already accepted an offer elsewhere. Today, he was planning to turn in his notice. He smiled because now he had the day off. Brendan "Slim" McNair always landed on his feet.

He didn't want to go home but didn't have anywhere to go. Everyone he knew was at work. He decided to go home to clean his apartment and do his laundry. After giving his apartment a thorough cleaning, he loaded every scrap of laundry into his truck. He was determined to make this week count. He planned to finish up the many household projects he'd started. Armed with about forty dollars in quarters, he drove the two miles to the nearest laundromat. As he unloaded his truck, he swore for the umpteenth time that he would invest in a washer and dryer soon.

Arriving before noon on a Monday gave him access to all the washers he needed. He got the clothes loaded and sat down. His stomach growled angrily, reminding him that a breakfast sandwich was all he'd eaten. He looked over at the vending machine and saw an "out of order" sign posted across the glass. He turned around just as a young girl walked in with a young child happily snacking on a bag of chips.

"If you want a snack, the hotel next door has a vending machine right inside the lobby," she said as she plopped down in a chair.

"Thanks," Slim said with a nod and headed out the door, lighting up a cigarette as he went.

It only took a few minutes to reach the hotel. Seeing the side entrance, he pulled on the door, but it didn't budge.

"You have to use your room key," said a feminine voice behind him.

He turned at the sound of her voice and was unable to move or speak. She was just that beautiful. Unlike the women he usually dated, this woman was obviously more mature. She was well dressed in a burgundy business suit with her hair pulled up into a stylish bun. The lady pulled a key out of her pocket and slid it through the slot. She tapped her nail on the "no smoking" sign before walking in.

Slim grabbed the door and put out the cigarette in the nearby ashtray. By the time he got through the door, she was gone. He walked through the lobby in hopes of finding the lady. After a few minutes, he gave up and went over to the vending machine to grab a few snacks to tide him over until later.

He walked back to the laundromat to find the young mother bopping her head to something on her iPod while her kid ran top speed up and down the aisles. The woman looked up and smiled at him. He noted she was cute. Her braided extensions swung as she moved. She had a pretty face and banging body—a combination that usually spelled trouble. He didn't need any more trouble.

He walked over to a chair and sat down. He still had a while before his clothes would be ready for the dryer. Slim scanned the magazines left on the table, finding them all boring. He selected a book from the pile of dusty books and began to read. Other people filed into the laundromat bringing the noise level up about seven notches.

He got up and transferred his clothes to the dryer and went to sit back down. About twenty minutes later, the cute girl from earlier sat down across from him and smiled, showing off a gold tooth and dimples. He nodded and went back to his book. He didn't want anything to do with her, so he turned slightly and started reading again. Obviously, she didn't understand his body language.

"Hi, my name is Rasheeda," she said extending her hand.

"Slim," was all he said and tried to get back into his book. Luckily, her kid needed attention, so she took him into the bathroom.

Slim got up and began loading his baskets and transporting them to the truck. Gathering the last two baskets, he looked over at Rasheeda, and she gave him a smile that said a lot. He knew that smile, and he knew that look. This time last year, he might have taken her up on her apparent offer. Every man had a type. She was definitely his.

Older and wiser now, he just shook his head as he looked at her one last time as he walked out the door. He had got burnt before by fooling around with a young chick. Never again. He was no longer looking for that type of woman.

***

Joy closed the door to her office, sat down, and leaned back in the leather office chair and tried to focus. Mondays were always busy. Weekend reports, as well as the day's reports, had to be done. Once she finished that, the schedules for next week had to be written. She didn't want her daydreaming about the man at the door to cause her to lose time. She tried to get the man out of her mind when suddenly the head housekeeper barged into her office waving her hands as she spoke. She was going a mile a minute, gushing over a man she saw walking towards the laundromat.

Joy's lips curled up into a smile as she remembered the guy she saw at the door. She knew from Sydney's description that she was talking about him. He was very nice to look at. The man had to be over six feet tall. He almost towered over her five foot seven inches. He was dark with a close-cropped haircut. Chocolate had always been her favorite flavor for men. 'A tall drink of water' as her mom would say.

Thinking about her workload, she shooed the young lady from her office. She had too much paperwork to do. The general manager was on vacation again, which meant not only did she have her own work to do but hers as well.

Even though the encounter was brief, it had left an impression. She thought about how he just stood there with a goofy look on his face. She knew he was checking her out. Her double Ds always demanded attention. She allowed herself to daydream for only a few minutes, then she drove him out of her mind. One disastrous marriage was enough. She looked down at her left hand and gazed at the huge rock she still wore. There was no man attached to the ring anymore. He had moved on and left her without so much as a backward glance. She called the ring her blocker since it made men think twice about asking her out.

Her best friend and one-time lover, Tristan, begged her to sell the ring and move on. She knew he was right, but she wasn't ready to even consider another man. She knew dating didn't have to lead to marriage, but even dating was scary right now. The good-looking man at the door made her second guess her decision. He was tall, dark and handsome just the way she liked them. She hadn't heard his voice but thought it would be deep and rich just like is skin. However, she didn't have time to agonize over it. She had work to do.

Joy worked steadily, and the time passed quickly. She let her mind drift a few times, and he was in her thoughts. Never had the sight of a man made her consider a relationship since her ex-husband. Just seeing this man made her want to run after him. That piece of eye candy made her think about all she had been missing.

***

Slim put the last of the laundry up and walked into the kitchen to start dinner. Thanks to his mother and grandmother, he was a great cook. He soon had the apartment smelling great. He turned on the radio and enjoyed a glass of wine. As soon as he got comfortable, there was a knock at the door.

His ex-wife, Tiffany, stood at the door wearing a spaghetti-strapped sundress and heels. Her hair was down the way he liked it. She had it parted down the middle framing her face. She gave him a sweet smile, and he remembered why he wanted her in the first place. Tiffany was naturally pretty. Her skin was the color of smooth cocoa. She even sported dimples. She was as they say a 'brick house.' She smiled seductively, letting him know she definitely wanted something.

"Is it true? Did you guys get laid off?" she asked as she walked into the room uninvited. "I have a trip planned this weekend," she continued.

"You will get your check," he said evenly.

"That's not what I want. I want to know if you can watch the kids. My mom can't babysit, and since you off I was wondering…"

The look on his face silenced her. Slim opened the door and looked back at her without saying a word. She took the hint and walked silently out of the apartment, knowing what it meant when Slim motioned for her to leave.

That's cool, Slim, she thought as she walked back to the car she'd borrowed. *Throw me out. I got something for your ass,* she mused bitterly.

Tiffany had another card to play. The girls' trip would have to wait. She knew how much Slim loved her son and thought she would be able to play on his emotions. Maybe she didn't have any more influence over him.

On the drive back, Tiffany thought about the past few years. Slim was good to her. He married her when she told him about the baby. He paid the bills and gave her money when she needed it. He was loyal and dependable.

Reggie, on the other hand, was not. She had a thing for him ever since high school. Even though he was with someone else, they would sneak around together the majority of their high school years. After high school, she wanted more, but he didn't. She thought she was over him until she ran into him at a party. She was dating Slim at the time. She felt Slim was more of a sugar daddy than a boyfriend.

After the party, she spent the night with Reggie with no feelings of guilt. They began seeing each other regularly shortly after that. When she got pregnant, she didn't know what to do. Reggie was fresh out of jail with no job, and she knew things would be rough. When Slim found out she was pregnant and asked her to marry him, she said yes. Now, she was stuck with two kids and a man that could barely keep the lights on.

***

Slim's evening was officially ruined. How dare she come and ask him to watch her kids? Kids that he once believed to be his. If you ever want to see a grown man cry, tell him that lie. Slim turned off the oven and took out his casserole. He grabbed his glass of wine then walked over to his easy chair and sat down. Then, he let the events of that dreadful day when he found out the truth replay in his mind.

Slim had gotten off early and went straight home. He opened the door expecting his toddler son to greet him with outstretched arms. Silence met him at the door. Confused, he walked through each room in the apartment. Tiffany's car was outside, so where could she be?

Assuming she was at a neighbor's, he started on dinner. The phone rang, but his hands were full, so the machine caught the call. Her friend, Trish's, voice filled the room. She wanted to know how long it would be before she came to get the baby. Suspicion took over Slim's emotions as he slid into a kitchen chair. Why would she need a sitter? She's not working due to being in her final six weeks of pregnancy, and why is her car here if our child is somewhere else? he wondered. He jumped up and went outside to move his truck to the back of the apartment complex. He came in the back door and walked over to the couch and sat down.

Tiffany came through the door smiling. She was talking to someone behind her. She turned around and came face to face with her husband. The look of guilt on her face said it all. Before she could speak or close the door, her lover came up behind her. Tiffany had left her purse in his car. They stared at each other for about a minute. Words were not necessary.

Slim left Tiffany that night. It was in court that he found out his son was not his. The child she was carrying came out looking so much like the other man that Slim didn't even bother to take a DNA test.

No need to dwell on it, he thought. *What's done is done.*

He couldn't change the past, but in the future, he would choose wisely. That beautiful woman he saw earlier had piqued more than his interest. Maybe that's what he needed. A nice, mature woman. He put Tiffany out of his mind and ate his dinner. After dinner, he loaded the dishwasher and called it a night.

Chapter 2

Tuesday morning promised to be a better day. Slim received a phone call from his new employer to confirm he would be in on Monday. His mother called immediately after that. She was in town and coming over. He was glad he had already cleaned his apartment. His mom arrived just in time for breakfast. He loved spoiling her, so he made all of her favorites. As they began to dig into the meal he cooked, he tilted his head to the side and said, "Okay Momma, who told you? It's Tuesday, so how did you know I was home?"

His mom could only laugh.

"Bootsey!" they said in unison.

Bootsey was the town gossip. She knew everything and everybody. According to his mom, Bootsey had called her and told her about the big lay off, so she had called him to see for herself.

"When you answered, I knew you had been laid off too," she said. There was a look of worry on her face.

He quickly eased her mind. "Mom, I have another job starting Monday."

With a look of relief, she stood and announced she wanted him to take her to Sam's.

"Yes ma'am," was all he said.

His mother lived about forty miles outside of town, so she went to Sam's about once a month for supplies to avoid going to the small overpriced local grocers. Happy to have some company this time, she tossed him the keys to her car.

Slim chuckled and walked around to the driver's side of the car. He looked over at his mom and smiled. He thought about how she worked to raise him all alone. She never complained; she just got the job done. He had no idea who his father was. After a while, he stopped asking her about him. He just hoped one day she would tell him. As for today, he was just glad to have her.

Arriving at the store, Slim slid into a parking spot close to the door. Once he'd let his mom out, he grabbed a shopping cart and followed her inside.

***

Joy finished her morning reports and started on the deposits from the day before. After she had balanced the shift reports, she made out the bank deposit slip and got ready to run to the bank.

"Okay, I'm headed to the bank, so send any calls to voicemail," she said to the desk clerk.

"Don't forget to go to Sam's," replied the clerk, handing her a list of office necessities. "And, don't forget that you have a conference call in an hour."

"Oh yeah, I better hurry!" said Joy.

Minutes later, Joy pulled up to the local Sam's after making the hotel bank deposit. According to her list, the hotel needed office and kitchen supplies. As she perused the aisle in search of the items she needed, she heard an intoxicatingly sexy voice coming from the aisle behind her. His words flowed smoothly as he conversed with a female. The conversation sounded like one between mother and son. She fought the urge to turn the corner. She wondered if he looked as good as he sounded. Taking a deep breath, she started down the aisle. She really didn't have much time.

She was forced to come to an abrupt halt as a cart turned down the aisle she was leaving. She came face to face with a smiling older female and *him*. The gorgeous man from yesterday was standing only a few feet away.

"So, we meet again," he said in his deep, baritone voice.

She was frozen for a moment. *The sexy voice belonged to him.*

"Yes, I guess so," she said.

"I never got a chance to introduce myself yesterday. My name is Brendan, Brendan McNair, but everybody calls me Slim."

"I'm Joy Spicer. Nice to meet you, Mr. McNair," she said.

"What's the rush?" he asked as he grabbed the end of her cart.

"I have to get back to the hotel. We need these supplies," she said, pointing to her cart.

"Oh, so you work there?"

"Yes, I do."

"Which hotel do you work for?" his mom asked, pushing him out of the way.

"I work at the inn right across the street."

"Oh really, the big one on the corner?" asked his mom as she moved him out of the way.

"Yes, ma'am."

"I was wondering if you had a conference or banquet room."

"Yes ma'am, we have both."

"Well great, I don't want to keep you, so do you have a card?"

"Yes ma'am," she said as she fished one out of her purse.

"Thank you. I'll be in touch."

Joy gave the pair a polite nod and walked away.

"Thank me later," said his mom as she handed him the card.

He smiled and placed the card in his pocket. His mom was smiling from ear to ear.

"Okay, mom," he said with a chuckle.

Joy couldn't help but think she had just got played. She wasn't mad about it 'cause the brother was fine. She shook her head and smiled thinking to herself, *okay, Brendan, the ball's in your court.*

Joy hurried to finish her shopping and leave the store. Once she got back to the hotel, it was time for her conference call. After the conference call, she got started on a project and completely forgot about the encounter. After work, she met up with some friends for shopping and dinner. The girls were talking about their kids, boyfriend, and husbands while she nodded and smiled.

She wanted to tell them about the man she just met but thought better of it. She wasn't sure herself what to make of him just yet. He was quite a looker, but she didn't know anything about him beyond his looks. *He may not even call. I could be worrying about nothing.*

She walked into her house a little after nine. It was too late to do anything except shower and head to bed. As soon as she got comfortable with the TV set on her favorite sitcom, the phone rang. She assumed it was her mother since no one else called her that late. "Yes ma'am, I am home, the door is locked, and the alarm is set," she said in a sing-song voice.

"Good to know," a deep, baritone voice responded.

"Excuse me? Who is this?" she asked with a lot of attitude.

"Slim."

She smiled in spite of herself. "Oh, what's up?" she asked trying to sound sexy.

The two ended up talking for hours. He was definitely not what she expected. The conversation never went left. He was a perfect gentleman. They talked about everything. She was surprised at how smoothly the conversation flowed. The hours went by quickly. Neither of them wanted to say goodnight.

***

Lying in bed after the call, Slim replayed the conversation in his head. He found her to be smart as well as beautiful. She was not like the other women he'd dated recently. After his divorce, he just ran through women. One night stands and friends with benefits were all he'd dealt with since his divorce. He was hurt and took it out on the women that followed Tiffany. This woman was different. She was much more than a casual roll in the hay. He realized he was dealing with a lady.

Slim's mother always told him to take his time when dealing with a lady. This time, he would listen. His mother had warned him about Tiffany, yet he married her anyway. Now, he was paying for it literally. He just wanted to leave her in the past.

Joy seemed to be just what he needed. He realized she was just as beautiful inside. It turned out their schedules clashed. Slim would be working second shift for a while, and Joy was assisting at another property out of town. She would be busy for a few weeks until the manager got back from vacation. They communicated only by telephone for a while. Even though it wasn't what he wanted, he felt it would give him time to get to know her.

***

Joy went to work on Wednesday with a smile on her face and a spring in her step. After one conversation, she was already smitten. Not once did she hear the old tired clichés most men used. He was obviously raised right. After a year of not dating, it was refreshing to have a conversation with someone that could be a potential mate. She completed her morning paperwork and was expected to travel to a sister property. Joy took advantage of the hour and a half drive and replayed the conversation in her head. She learned a lot about him in those few hours. She couldn't wait to talk to him again.

After she got to the hotel, she busied herself with reports and time moved quickly. A sudden downpour made her change her mind about driving back, so she checked into a room. After a brief conversation with her mother, she called her best friend, Portia.

"Hey girl," said Portia."

"What are you doing?"

"Joy, we just hung out last night, so what's up?"

"Girl, you know me too well."

"That I do."

"I met someone."

"When? Why didn't you tell us last night."

"I met him yesterday, and we didn't get a chance to talk until after I left you guys."

"Oh, okay. So, tell me about him. I know he gotta be fine. Where does he work? What kind of money does he make?"

"Whoa, slow down. We only had one conversation, but he used to work at Evans. He starts at Newell next week."

"A plant?" Portia replied in a disapproving tone.

"Yes, Portia. He works in a plant. What is wrong with that?"

"Nothing, I guess. So, how many kids?"

"None, Portia."

"Okay, that's a plus. Has he ever been married?"

"Yes."

"Looks like you're trying something new. Well, I guess you really don't have time to be too choosy," she said with a soft chuckle.

"Ma'am, we are the same age, and you are single too. I have been married before. Can you say the same?"

"Excuse me! I didn't mean to offend."

Joy let out a long sigh and rolled her eyes to the ceiling before saying, "Portia, I'll talk to you later." She disconnected the call as Portia's insensitive comments put a slight damper on her mood.

Joy's ex-husband was rich, good looking, and a graduate of an ivy league college, but where was he now? She loved Portia like a sister and usually valued her opinion, but her friend was becoming a snob.

Minutes later, Joy answered the phone and heard Slim's deep, baritone voice say, "Hello, pretty lady." That was all she needed to hear to make her smile again.

They spoke on the phone every day for the rest of the week. She wanted to see him again, but work made it impossible. She would have to cover a few shifts when she came back into town. She was pleasantly surprised when he showed up at the hotel.

"Hi, pretty lady."

"Hi," she said with a wide grin.

"I just wanted to lay eyes on you."

Joy shyly dropped her head.

He tilted her head up and kissed her lightly on the lips. "I have to go, but I'll call you later. Okay?

"I'll be looking forward to it," she said and watched him walk out of the door.

His cologne, his walk, his voice all had her floating on air. She made a silent plea to the powers that be. *Please let him be the one.*

After several weeks of phone calls, Slim was finally able to have her over for dinner. They agreed on the upcoming Friday. He frequently stopped by to see her, but the ten-minute visits weren't enough. Now that he was working day shift again, he was finally going to spend some real time with her. Slim got off early on Friday and rushed home to prepare. He grabbed the mail from the box and threw it on the coffee table. He chopped the veggies and seasoned the meat in preparation for the dinner. After a refreshing shower, he dressed for the evening.

Joy was definitely impressed. His small apartment was neat and clean. It was definitely a man's place. Soft leather furniture in shades of brown filled the room. She made herself comfortable on the sofa as he put the finishing touches on dinner.

"This is great. Who taught you how to cook?" she asked in between bites.

"My mom and my grandma had a hand in teaching me."

"They did a great job," she said. "You should cater."

"Thanks. I used to complain about cooking, but now I'm glad I paid attention. I actually enjoy it."

"There is nothing wrong with that."

"Well, there is plenty so please help yourself."

"I will do just that," she said with a wink.

Slim hoped her statement had a double meaning.

After the meal, the couple relaxed on the sofa. Slim didn't want to push her or make her feel uncomfortable, but he desperately wanted to make love to her. The phone conversations were good, but seeing her in person again was making it hard for him to keep his hands to himself. He kissed her tenderly and slowly ended the kiss. *Slow,* he was thinking. *I don't want to ruin this by going too fast.*

Joy had other things on her mind, and she let him know it. Joy grabbed his hands and placed them on her breasts. He didn't have to be told twice. Having been celibate for the last year made Joy more than ready to break the fast. Slim stood and pulled her into standing position. He placed his hands on her waist and guided her through the archway that led to his bedroom.

Slim begin by kissing her neck and shoulders as he undressed her. Her body was beautiful. He took time to admire her thighs and full breasts. She urged him to hurry by grabbing his sex. They came together with a sense of urgency. The passion was beyond what either had experienced before. Exhaustion finally made them stop. After a well-deserved nap, they began again, this time slower.

Joy woke first. She looked over at him and gently stroked his face. She was falling for him, and it scared her. Slim reached out for her in his sleep and pulled her into his arms. That small act soothed her, and she soon fell asleep again. Slim woke a little while later and made breakfast. This time, the smell of bacon woke her.

Over breakfast, they talked and realized they both had the weekend off. They made plans to spend the weekend together. Their phone conversations were great but being together was much better. Joy hurried home to get a few changes of clothes and toiletries. The way their schedule worked, it could be a while before they had the weekend off together again.

Joy returned to find Slim sitting on the small porch smoking a cigarette.

"Hey," she said with a smile at the sight of him. But as she got closer, she saw the look of distress on his face.

When she stepped on to the porch, he jumped. He was so deep in thought that he didn't hear her walk up. "Hey, I didn't hear you come up," he said.

"What's wrong?" asked Joy.

He pointed to a pile of mail. "My ex-wife is suing me for child support."

"How is she suing for child support? I thought you didn't have any children."

"The baby was born before we divorced. Tiffany put my name on the birth certificate. I should have known she would try something. She just got her final alimony check. Now, she's trying to get another check!"

"Okay, but if the baby isn't yours, how can they make you pay child support?"

"I never took a DNA test for her, but I don't believe she is mine. But it is a possibility."

"Just take the test and find out the truth. Then, we will go from there."

He smiled. Slim realized she didn't say *you*. She said *we* and that small little word let him know they were in this together.

"Yeah," he said and let out an exasperated breath. "I'm so tired of her. I just want to be done with that woman."

"You are done with that woman," she said and planted a kiss on his lips.

He knew he made the right choice. He felt Joy truly cared for him, not just looking for what she could get *from* him.

Joy took the letter out of his hand. "Let's not let this letter affect our first weekend together," she said. "We have had two days alone, and we're going to use them."

"I like the way you think," Slim said and pulled her back in for another kiss.

The new couple spent the weekend laughing and enjoying each other's company. The lovemaking was intense and satisfying. For the next two days, they only came up for air when necessary.

Chapter 3

The following Monday Joy had to attend a conference. She chose to drive the four hours instead of flying to the conference. The first seminar wasn't until Tuesday morning. She purposely arrived early enough to do some shopping. She felt like a little retail therapy was in order. Once she checked into the hotel and unpacked her car, she headed to the large outlet mall a few miles away.

Joy was quite familiar with the city. Her ex-husband's family lived there, and they visited quite a bit when they were together. She visited her favorite shops first. Then, she roamed the mall in search of deals. With her shopping done, she decided to stop at the food court for a soft pretzel.

As she munched and walked towards the parking lot, she thought she heard her name being called. She turned but didn't see any familiar faces, so she proceeded on out the door. She pressed the unlock button for the trunk of her car and dropped her purchases in. She closed the trunk and started to the driver's side of her car only to come face to face with her ex-husband, Morris.

"I thought that was you! What are you doing in town?" he asked. He even had the nerve to smile.

Instantly angry, she replied, "Why are you here in my face? MOVE!" She shoved past him and quickly unlocked the door and entered her car. She drove away without a backward glance. Later, after she cooled off, she ordered take-out thinking *diet be damned. How dare he even speak to me like nothing ever happened?*

Morris had watched her back out of parking space and drive away. His heart sank. He was so overjoyed when he realized it was her that he momentarily forgot the breakup. Walking out on his wife was the worst mistake he had made to date. Slowly, he walked back to his own vehicle and started the engine. There was no need to follow her. He had an idea as to where she was headed. He desperately wanted to talk to her but knew she would not allow it. He didn't blame her one bit. An apology wouldn't be enough, and he knew it.

Morris drove to the hotel he knew her company used for meetings. A meeting would be the only reason for her being in town, he surmised. He watched her park, unload her car and walk into the building. He wanted to go after her and beg for her forgiveness, but his pride wouldn't let him. Wistfully, he gave his ex-wife one last look then backed out of the parking space and started for home.

He pulled into his driveway and killed the engine. The apartment was void of sound. Bland colored walls and dull furniture stared back at him. He dropped his keys on the table and slumped down into a nearby chair. The sparse furnishing and lack of décor belied his financial status as the apartment contained essentials only. One wrong move had placed him in this predicament. Having a beautiful wife wasn't enough for him. Lust and greed lured him away from her.

Giving into temptation, he went home with a woman he'd been eyeing for some time. Cheating on his wife wasn't planned, but once he did, the excitement of the act couldn't be matched. It was like a drug to him. Once he got started, he couldn't stop. The women became an obsession. Most of his business trips had nothing to do with business.

After awakening in a strange bed with people he didn't know, he knew things had to change. He went home and looked at the home he'd turned his back on. He didn't deserve her. He filed for a divorce and never went back. He knew he had taken the coward's way out, but he could not face her. He could not face himself. Morris had convinced himself he was doing what was best for her by leaving.

Now, he was alone. He wished he had the chance to talk to her. His time was short, so he was tying up loose ends. With all the women he'd slept with, he thought he was lucky that HIV didn't claim him. However, cancer did.

He knew his life expectancy was less than a few months. He had liquidated the majority of his assets and had his Will revised. He made sure everything went to

Joy. She never did anything to deserve what he did to her. He couldn't turn back the hands of time. The only way he felt he could rest in peace was to let her know how much he loved her.

He sat down at the cheap table that came with the apartment and wrote a letter, confessing everything he did during their marriage. He begged her to forgive him. He sealed it and enclosed it in the large envelope along with the instructions. He had a messenger arriving soon to take the paperwork to his lawyer.

With that done, he felt he had completed all that he needed to. Now all he had to do was wait on the disease to claim him.

***

Joy plopped down on her bed and noticed the message light was blinking on the phone. She dialed zero to reach the front desk. The clerk relayed her messages. Slim had called while she was out. She smiled at the thought of him. They had only been together a short while, and things were still new. She knew there weren't any guarantees in relationships. This time, she would keep her eyes open.

Schedule conflicts made it easy to keep things from moving too fast. The phone conversations allowed them to talk long hours and get to know each other on a deeper level. She felt good about him. She felt his intentions were honorable. The main drawback was his ex-wife, Tiffany. *What if the baby is his?* She didn't want to deal with 'baby Momma drama.' Getting involved with a man in that type of situation could be very stressful. She had to realistic. Finding a man without children at their age was almost impossible. She wanted to give the relationship a chance, even though she knew a crazy ex could put a real strain on a relationship. She sighed and thought it was too early to even worry about it. She decided time would tell if she needed to cut and run.

Oblivious to the fact that Morris had followed her, Joy went about her business. The next few days were busy for her. The company was implementing new procedures she would have to train her staff on when she returned. She took notes and immersed herself in her work. She went to all of the company dinners and had actually enjoyed herself.

Glad the conference was over, she loaded her car and got on the road. She got home midday on Friday. After she unloaded her car, she decided to soak away the trip in a nice hot bubble bath. She dried off and applied lotion to her body. She sat on the side of her king size poster bed and fantasized about her upcoming date with Slim. Her phone rang snapping her out of the daydream.

"Hello."

"Hey girl, I have news that I have to tell you face to face," said her friend Portia in an excited tone.

"Okay girl, come on over. I was just about to order some food."

"I'll be there in a few," Portia said and disconnected the call.

Joy slipped into a pair of shorts and a tee shirt. She called to her favorite Chinese restaurant and ordered enough food for her and Portia. She felt that unpacking wouldn't take long, so she started on it until her food and Portia arrived.

She started hanging up her new clothes and thought about her encounter with Morris. The tears came out of nowhere. The last time she saw her estranged husband was the day before her birthday. They were making plans for the weekend. He went to work the next day and never came home. She got served with divorce papers a few days later. *That's over and done with now,* she reminded herself then quickly washed her face. She didn't want Portia to see her like that.

Portia arrived about twenty minutes later. She walked through the door with her left hand extended.

"He proposed!" announced Portia.

The two ladies embraced and then gleefully danced around the room until Joy heard a knock at the door. She was glad to have a distraction. She went to pay the deliveryman all the while thinking Portia was about to make a huge mistake.

The two ladies chatted about Portia's upcoming nuptials over Chinese food. Joy wasn't really happy for her friend, though she smiled at how happy Portia seemed. They talked about venues, menus, and the number of bridesmaids there would be. She wanted a traditional wedding, and of course, she wanted Joy to help her plan it. With all that was going on at work, Joy barely had time to date, let alone plan a wedding.

Joy felt nothing but dread about the upcoming nuptials. The man Portia was marrying didn't seem ideal. She knew about the highs and lows of marriage. Portia was only looking at dollar signs. However, when she looked at her excited friend, she agreed to help with the wedding.

Seeing Portia happy changed her mind about helping out, but did she want to do something like that again? Could she get married again? She had been asking herself that question for months. She had to admit that Slim had her thinking about it.

***

More often than not, Slim thought about Joy the week she had to attend the conference. The week moved slowly for him. Saturday couldn't come fast enough. He took the time to think about the last year. It had been very hard for him. The divorce was bad, but the most devastating thing was finding out that his son wasn't his. Obviously, she had been cheating on him the whole time even before they got married. He also realized he really wanted a family. He felt like he had done the right thing by marrying Tiffany. He knew she was twelve years his junior, but he thought she would settle down once she had the baby.

Slim had been so busy working and trying to support his new family he didn't see the signs. Tiffany just wanted the money and security that came with being married, not an actual husband. Slim was so happy to have a son he ignored too much. He was glad to be divorced from Tiffany. He loved his 'son,' and it hurt like hell to have to leave him. Being that he was still a toddler, it wouldn't take long for the child to forget him. It would be much longer for Slim.

His mother had warned him about Tiffany. She even stopped speaking to him for a while. He still remembered the conversation he and his mother had the night he told her about their upcoming nuptials.

"Tiffany's pregnant, Mom. We're getting married."

"Son, are you sure? Are you even sure the baby is yours? You guys have only been together for a few months."

"Yes, Mom, I know. But I don't want my child to be born out of wedlock."

"She's wild, and I don't trust her. You're a grown man, but I'm your mother so I can give you my opinion. She's just too young and too hood. She's not going to change. I know you want to do the honorable thing, but she's not ready for the type of commitment marriage takes."

"Mom, we are getting married. If you want to come, it will be at her church the last Saturday of the month. The reception will be there as well."

"Slim, that girl is a common hoochie. Remember son, you cannot turn a 'ho' into a housewife."

Slim held his tongue for a while, but when he finally spoke it ended the conversation. "Mother, I don't want my child growing up not knowing his or her father like I did. I am marrying her."

His mother knew she couldn't change his mind or argue with the fact that she never told him about his father. She disconnected the call. Not only did she not show up to the wedding, but his mother also did not speak to him for months after that.

He switched his thoughts back to Joy. He knew her mostly through phone conversations. He wanted to know her better. He wanted to know what she was like day to day. For the first time, he was truly intrigued by a woman. Not trapped by a woman. He wanted to know what Joy liked and disliked, from her favorite foods to her deepest fears.

Finally Saturday, Slim closely followed the directions Joy gave him to her house. He knew from the address she lived in a ritzy neighborhood. The further he drove, the scenery around him changed drastically. He made his final right turn and found himself in a very upscale neighborhood. He was a bit apprehensive now. Slim had always been a confident man, but what could he really offer this woman?

He parked and started towards the door. He took in the landscaping and surrounding houses. He saw manicured lawns with carefully trimmed hedges. When Joy opened the door, she stood in front of him in a flirty pink dress that fit her like a glove. The dress was low cut but tastefully so. The shade of pink was very complimentary to the color of her skin.

He smiled at the sight of her. "You look great! Too good for the movies."

"Thank you, you look nice too. Come on in."

He entered the house and couldn't help but notice the décor. He looked around at the expensive furniture and trimmings. This woman would not need him like the women of his past. She had her own. She sensed he wasn't comfortable.

"Brendan, what's the matter?"

"What could I ever give you that you don't already have?"

"What do you mean?"

"Men want to feel needed," he said while looking around the room. The male in him was threatened. He was used to being the provider. She definitely didn't need him to provide.

Joy watched his reaction to the house and realized what he meant. She looked at him and spoke the one word that ended his trepidation. "You."

That was all he needed to hear. The tension was erased. He was with someone that wanted him, not what he could give them. He pulled her into his arms and kissed her tenderly. They were dangerously close to falling in love. He felt it. She felt it. They never made it to the movies.

Two days were spent mostly in her bedroom. Sunday afternoon they came up for air. Limbs intertwined and unabashedly nude, the couple sipped on wine and listened to music.

"Let's go and get some ice cream," she said, sitting up in the middle of the bed.

He shook his head and chuckled. "Okay, put some clothes on, and we can go."

The simple things were all she ever asked him for. That was another thing he loved about her. She was never demanding or overbearing. He was happy to take her anywhere she wanted to go. The quick trip to the ice cream shop turned out to be the beginning of a turnaround for Slim. On the way back to the car, a male voice yelled out his name.

"Slim McNair!"

Slim turned at the sound of his name. Grinning, he greeted his cousin Junior.

"Hey man, what's going on?

"Nothing much. Just work. I've been trying to get in touch with you." Junior looked over at Joy and tried not to stare. "And who is this young lady?"

"This is Joy. She's my lady," Slim stated, putting emphasis on the word my.

"Nice to meet you," Junior said, extending his hand. Joy shook his hand, and he held it a bit too long.

Slim cleared his throat, and Junior dropped her hand like it was on fire.

"So, what are you trying to reach me for? What's going on?" asked Slim.

"Well," he started but looked at Joy and hesitated.

Joy picked up on it. "I will wait in the car," she said, taking the keys from Slim.

Joy sat in the car and started in on her ice cream. She looked up at the two men talking and saw Slim wasn't happy about whatever his friend was telling him. She waited and watched for a few minutes. They walked further from the car as they spoke. Whether it was intentional or not, she didn't know. She didn't want to doubt Slim, but this time she would keep her eyes opened.

Slim got in the car and started the engine. He didn't mention the conversation, and neither did she. He was quiet on the way to her house. Once they arrived, Slim said, "I need to get home. I'll call you later tonight."

Joy didn't press him. She allowed him to kiss her and got out of the car. She stood in the walkway and watched him drive away.

Once he was out of sight, she got into her car and drove off in the opposite direction. A few minutes later, she pulled up into her friend Tristan's driveway. The negative comments she'd gotten from Portia made her decide against calling her. She felt dejected and needed her friend. He opened the door wearing sweat pants and a tee shirt.

"Hey Tristan, sorry to disturb your workout."

"What's wrong?" he asked as he ushered her into the living room while drying his face with the towel around his neck. He left her on the sofa and went to retrieve wine and two glasses. He sat down next to her and placed an arm around her shoulder. "Just let it out. Tell me."

"I thought we had a good start. The majority of our relationship has been by phone. We can talk about anything. He has always been open with me. Then, his ex-wife started causing him grief. She is after him for child support," Joy said after she took her first sip of wine.

"Okay," Tristan said, still waiting for the other shoe to drop.

"Wait! That's not really it. Today, we went out to get ice cream and ran into one of his friends. They walked off and had a private conversation, and my gut tells me that it's trouble."

"Why do you feel that it may be trouble?"

"I just do. When he got back into the car, he didn't say a word. He drove me home and left. He just left. He just wasn't himself. I thought we were closer than that. I don't know why he didn't just tell me what was going on."

"Just break it off," Tristan said in a flat tone.

"Tristan!" she exclaimed in a frustrated voice.

"You really like him?" he asked.

"Yeah, and I am scared as hell."

Tristan pulled her into his arms and let her cry. He tried to soothe her and let her know he would always be there. "It may be nothing to worry about. You two just got together. Give him time to come and talk to you."

"Something is not right, Tristan. I feel it," she said in a shaky voice.

They drank wine and talked until she fell asleep. Tristan looked down at her sleeping peacefully. He rubbed her back and thought about the brief love affair they

Slim and the Lady

shared. They had been friends for years before they crossed the line. When she decided she only wanted them to be friends, he agreed. He thought she would come around eventually, so he kept things friendly. He never told her she still had his heart. He stroked her hair and thought about the years they spent together.

He met her when she was about twelve. At first, she was just a chubby, nerdy neighbor. Their friendship developed slowly. By the time they were in high school, they were very close. Being older, he left for college a year earlier than she did. When he saw her again, she was jaw-droppingly gorgeous. He begged her to attend the same college. He had always loved her, but it wasn't until she broke up with him that he realized he was *in love* with her. Tristan hoped to get a chance to be with her again. Being friends was okay, but he couldn't deal with her being in love with another man. Not again.

***

Slim got home and thought about the brief conversation he had with Junior. Could things get any worse? First, Tiffany with her issues, and now this. How much more could he take? The past year was coming back to haunt him. After he left Tiffany, he was careless and reckless. He was really in a bad place. He walked into the kitchen to pour himself a drink. But once he grabbed the bottle and opened it, he poured the contents down the drain. Every bottle of booze in the house got the same treatment.

"No more alcohol," he said out loud. "I stop drinking today."

After he ridded the house of liquor, he called his mom and told her about the conversation with Junior. "Mom, we need to talk."

"What's wrong, son?"

"I've got a situation." He took a deep breath before saying, "I think I am about to be a father."

"What! You two work fast."

"No, Mom, not Joy."

"What?! Start from the beginning, Brendan."

"Last year I met a lady, and we were together briefly. According to Junior, she is pregnant by me."

"What do you mean, according to Junior. Why don't you know for sure?"

"She lives in his home town. I met her after partying one night."

"What did Joy have to say?"

"I haven't told her."

"Well, son, this is really a tough one. But I'm always here if you need me."

"Thanks, Mom."

She listened and didn't judge. She told him she would be supportive and would help any way she could. He was glad she didn't jump down his throat. He didn't need her mad at him.

If he really had a child on the way, he wondered how Joy would take it. How would he maintain a relationship with his child who lives over a hundred miles away? How would he deal with Vanessa? There were so many questions running around in his head. He really wanted a drink, but he refused to let alcohol rule his life anymore. Drinking and partying had caused enough problems. He was a grown man, and it was about time to act like one. He was determined to take control of his life. Thirty-eight years old was past old enough to know better.

He never wanted a child born out of wedlock. Having so many unanswered questions about his own father made him even more determined to be there for any child he may have—children he'd wanted to have with Joy.

If it was true that he was already a father, he couldn't do anything to change it, so he would just have to deal with it. He sat down and tried to gather his thoughts. He wanted to tell Joy what was going on. He almost told her in the car. She looked so cute eating her ice cream. Things were going great with Joy, and he didn't want to bring any unnecessary negativity.

He could kick himself for being so careless. Joy had to know something was wrong. He should not have left so abruptly. But he needed to think. How was he going to deal with this if it were true?

He decided he would tell her after he was sure. If this thing turned out to be true, he hoped his relationship with Joy could survive the blow. In his heart, he knew he was in love with her. Even though the relationship was still new, he couldn't imagine life without her.

Chapter 4

Vanessa tried to get comfortable on the sofa, but being in the final stages of pregnancy made it hard. She rubbed her protruding belly and smiled. She only had a few weeks to go. Her family was very supportive of her decision to keep the baby. She had to admit she thought it was going to be World War III when her family found out. She knew that at her age it was not easy to get pregnant. She didn't want to be a single mom, but this was the card life had dealt. She was not happy about how the child was conceived. The father was still unaware of the impending birth of his daughter. She did make efforts to reach him, but people that don't want to be found aren't found.

Her main concern was having a healthy child. Truthfully, she could not be happier. At forty-three, she never thought it would happen for her. She couldn't believe it when the doctor told her she was pregnant. It was time for her yearly physical, and the nurse wanted to run a pregnancy test because she was a few weeks late. She didn't want the pregnancy test and was sure the results would be negative. The nurse did the test anyway explaining it was routine. She was so busy scanning the latest issue of Cosmo that she didn't even see the nurse smiling at the results.

Later, when the doctor gave her the results, she was so happy that she cried hysterically for almost fifteen minutes. Thanks to her half-brother the nursery was all set. He came over, assembled the crib, painted the walls and retiled the floor. The baby shower her mom and sister threw for her was a godsend. Her friends and family brought everything she needed. She only needed to keep a steady supply of pampers.

She slowly rose from the sofa to make yet another trip to the bathroom. After her restroom break, she walked through the nursery. She smiled at how beautiful the room turned out. Her brother did a great job transforming her spare room. The soft pastel colors and curtains finished the look. Everything was ready for her little girl's arrival.

She let her mind drift back to the weekend of her daughter's conception. At first, she chided herself for going out with and then sleeping with a man she barely knew. It was not like her. Doing the things she did those weeks was way out of character. But he was so damn sexy. Her body took over, and her mind couldn't stop it. Slim turned out to be a great lover. After their first few dates, she hoped to have a real relationship with him. She felt like she was in love and tried to let him know it. Now, she wanted him to be with her and their daughter. She hadn't seen him in months and was beginning to believe she wouldn't see him again.

Seeing his friend Junior in town was a lucky fluke. He wouldn't give her any information but promised her that he would have Slim contact her. *Just like a man,* she thought. They will protect a friend to the end. She could only hope Junior kept his word and Slim would contact her. This baby needed a father, and she wanted that man.

***

Slim decided to take the upcoming weekend and see for himself. He wanted to be face to face with her. He told Joy he needed to go out of town and check on his mother. He promised he would call her. Lying to her was hard to do. But until he was sure, he didn't want to say anything.

He planned to leave work early on Friday to get there before dark. He was sure of the way to town but was a bit sketchy on how to get to her house. Junior had given him the general directions to her neighborhood.

Honestly, he vaguely remembered Vanessa, and now he may be having a child with her. Those weekends spent out of town with Junior were crazy. They spent the majority of the time in strip clubs and at house parties. He felt ashamed about how he acted during that time. The way things ended with Tiffany really made him lose his mind for a while.

He could admit that she was beautiful and attractive. He met her at a diner one morning after a night of all night partying. She was nice looking, and he felt a little lucky. After getting her number, he promised to see her that weekend. He didn't even think Vanessa knew his real name, at least he didn't remember telling her. He slept with her several times over two months. He was always careful, but they did have a few condom mishaps. He knew that her being pregnant was a strong possibility.

Whatever happened, he wanted to make sure he did everything he could to secure his relationship with Joy. He'd finally found the right woman to build a life with, and now his past mistakes were trying to wreck it. He just had to deal with the consequences of his actions. If she was pregnant, and if it was his child, he knew things with Joy would be complicated. For that reason, he hoped she would understand that he wanted to be there for the child only. In his heart, he was already committed to Joy.

He remembered some of the conversations with Vanessa and knew she wanted more than he was willing to give. When she kept pressuring him, he stopped seeing her. He cut off all contact and changed his number. Vanessa didn't understand the only thing he wanted from her he'd had.

Slim drove into town around three in the afternoon. He found the neighborhood without any trouble but couldn't remember which house was hers. After circling the block a few times, he was about to give up when he saw her walking out of the door with a small rolling suitcase. He pulled up to the house and jumped out of the car.

"Vanessa?"

"Slim! My water broke!" she said and doubled over in pain.

Without a word, he grabbed her, carried her to the car, and threw the suitcase in the backseat. His heart was racing. With her giving directions, they got to the hospital in record time. After he signed her in, they got her settled into a room. In between contractions, he was able to have a long overdue conversation.

"Why didn't you contact me?"

"How could I contact you? The number you gave me didn't work. I knew your town but not your address. I don't even know your legal first name, *Slim.*"

"Vanessa, it was a fling, that's all. We didn't plan on this. I was going through a divorce, and you know it. We agreed to no strings attached. I told you up front that I was not looking for a relationship."

"That was then. We have a child now. We have a responsibility to her."

"I will be there for her, but please understand that I need a DNA test."

"I have no problem with that. We can get it done here before you leave." She looked at him and added, "Slim, this is your daughter."

"Brendan," he replied.

"What?"

"My name is Brendan McNair."

"It's nice to finally meet you."

With a smile, he reached out and shook her hand. They spent the night talking until the pain became too intense for her to continue. Being there for the birth was not planned, but he was glad he was there. He stayed by her side throughout the night and held her hand when it got rough. The baby finally arrived a little after two in the morning. Slim couldn't stop staring at the small brown face. The kid had him wrapped around her finger already. He believed the baby was his, but a DNA test was still ordered. Vanessa insisted on naming the baby after him.

"Welcome to the world, Brenda McNair," she whispered to her precious newborn.

Vanessa was truly enjoying motherhood. During her stay at the hospital, she was showered with gifts. Family members and friends showed up with gifts and well wishes. Balloons and cards crowded the small room. Vanessa thoroughly enjoyed the attention.

She smiled to herself as she thought about how Slim showed up just in time. Having him there at their daughter's birth meant everything to her. What a great way for her family to meet him. She was overjoyed at the fact of having a gorgeous hunk sitting in the room with her. *Not bad for a never married, forty-three-year-old woman,* she thought. She knew her friends were jealous.

Slim was polite to everyone but not overly talkative. He was helpful with the baby all day. He changed diapers and all. Seeing this side of him reaffirmed her feelings for him. She knew he didn't want a relationship before, but now there was a child involved. She had to admit that she did not know him that well. Their relationship was very brief, but she did let him know how she felt. At the time, he was adamant about not getting serious. She was sure she would be able to change his mind. After all, she was the mother of his child.

Vanessa looked down at the beautiful baby and whispered, "Your daddy will be with us, just you wait and see." She patted the baby's back as she hummed a lullaby.

Later that afternoon, Vanessa's sister, Carolyn, walked into the room with a big teddy bear. She leaned in for a hug and stopped short when she saw Slim sitting next to the window holding the baby. Even though over twenty years had passed, she knew it was him. He had grown into a handsome man. He was no longer tall and lanky but solid and dangerously sexy.

Vanessa smiled and thought about how jealous Carolyn must be, but Carolyn was not jealous, she was surprised. Vanessa had no idea her sister and her child's father knew each other quite well.

"This is Brendan, Brenda's father," she said to her sister then turned to him and said, "This is my sister, Carolyn."

Slim didn't speak right away; he simply stared. After all this time, she'd hardly aged at all.

"Hello, Carolyn. It's nice to meet you," he said, extending his free hand.

Not noticing the tension, Vanessa chimed in, "Yeah, this is my younger sister."

He handed the baby over to her mother. "I'll let you two visit. I need a cigarette."

Slim hurriedly walked out of the room. Carolyn sat down and forced a smile onto her face and thought to herself, *It's a small world after all.* The one person she thought she would never see again in life was only a few feet away. The ache she hadn't felt in over twenty years slowly began to take hold of her. She fought back her tears and reached out to hold her brand new niece.

***

Joy waited by the phone all weekend, but there were no calls from Slim. A week went by and still nothing. She refused to call him. She had given him the benefit of the doubt until she saw his mom in Sam's Monday morning. Brendan McNair had lied to her.

Joy fished out her blocker and put it back on her finger. She went back to wearing her hair up in a bun. She spoke only when spoken to and reserved smiles for the hotel guests. She didn't take calls from her friends nor did she go out. She went straight home from work every day that week.

Sunday, Slim showed up at her house. She hadn't seen or heard from him in days. She let him stand outside and knock. When the knocking stopped, she looked out the window and saw him sitting on her steps. She deserved an explanation, so she opened the door.

"I was going to sit here all night if I had to," he said.

"Come in," she said while moving to let him in.

"I owe you an explanation, I know that." Slim took a deep breath. "I have a daughter," he blurted.

"So the baby *is* yours?"

"Yes. No, I mean, not with Tiffany."

"Excuse me?" Joy asked, cocking her head to the side and putting her hands on her hips.

"Please, hear me out and let me explain," he pleaded. "Look, before I met you, I did a lot of things I'm not proud of. I was with a woman briefly. Her name is Vanessa. She got pregnant. I had no idea. I went to talk to her and pulled up to her house as she was walking out the door on the way to the hospital. Everything happened so fast. I stayed until the baby came. I took the DNA test, and I should get the results back next week. I wanted to tell you that day in the car, but I didn't want to say anything until I was sure."

"Why didn't you call me, Brendan? No," she shouted with her finger pointed at him. "Why didn't you trust me enough to tell me what was going on? If we are together, you cannot lie or hide things from me."

"You are right. I didn't want to lose you, and I panicked."

"She got pregnant before we met, right?"

"Yes."

"Then, we just have to work it out."

Relieved he hadn't lost her, he pulled her into his arms.

Joy narrowed her eyes and stepped back out of his embrace "Okay, that explains the weekend. What about all last week?"

Slim walked over and sat down on the sofa and covered his face with his hands.

"Joy, I just needed time to think. After she gave birth, I found out some more disturbing news."

Joy sensed he needed to get something else off his chest. She sat by him and laid her head on his shoulder. Slim took a deep breath before he spoke.

"The summer that I had just turned fifteen I went to spend the summer with my aunt. Me and my cousin Junior had planned to hang out and party. I met a girl named Carolyn the first week there at a house party. Man, I couldn't get enough of this girl. She was all that I thought about. Well anyway, on the fourth of July, we ended up alone somehow and, being teenagers, one thing led to another, and that was my first time.

"I thought I was in love. We started sneaking around, and one night she convinced me to come over saying her mom worked until ten. I started going over whenever I could sneak out. After a few times of not getting caught, I got too relaxed. We fell asleep, and her mom found us butt naked in Carolyn's bed. That woman beat my natural black ass. She called my aunt who called my mom and then I got beat again! My mom came and got me the next day. I tried to call and write to Carolyn for weeks. I finally gave up. My cousin said she left school after Christmas break. I never saw Carolyn again until last weekend."

Joy did not speak. She looked up at him waiting for him to continue.

"Carolyn is Vanessa's younger sister."

Joy's jaw dropped.

"Does Vanessa know?" she asked when she found her voice again.

"I don't know. I never met her until last year. Vanessa is older than us. She would have been grown at the time. She must have been in college or something."

"I don't want to sound selfish, but look at the situation you are asking me to walk into. You have a history with one sister and a child with the other. This could be a problem."

"I know, and that's why I needed time. I just needed a few days to sort things out in my head. I feel like I finally found the right one, and now everything from my past is coming back to haunt me." He gave her a pleading look.

Joy let out a long sigh and leaned in and kissed him. "I know all this happened before we met, so you and I will have to just roll with the punches. I truly appreciate the fact that you are being totally honest with me."

"I love you," he said with sincerity.

Joy allowed him to kiss her, but she couldn't help but think about the drama they may face with these women. She prayed that Tiffany's baby wasn't his, as well.

She wasn't ready to deal with 'baby Momma drama' let alone from two different women.

Slim promised himself he would make every effort to fix things with Joy. He knew Brenda's arrival changed things irrevocably. Dividing his time between Joy and the baby would be a challenge. He wanted to devise a feasible plan that would work for all concerned. Vanessa wasn't a problem yet, but he felt she might be later on.

Then, there was Carolyn. How did he not know she had a sister? Did Vanessa know about him and Carolyn? It was over twenty years ago, but some things are not easily forgotten.

***

Returning home from the hospital, Vanessa felt a bit depressed. After having Slim at the hospital, she was sure he would bring her home. Instead, her sister, Carolyn, did. Vanessa had Slim's mobile number, so she felt a little better about that. Her mother missed the birth altogether. She was on a singles cruise. That also added to Vanessa's melancholy. She placed her newborn in the newly refurbished crib and took a seat in the rocker.

Vanessa had always been a planner. She wrote everything down. Agendas and to-do lists were religiously written in her blue notebook. She started on a new outline for her new plan of action. She had a goal in mind—Slim. Before he left, he gave her his cell number and address. She promptly added him to her contacts as Hubby. She planned to have him and have him soon.

Brenda started to cry, but before Vanessa could get up, Carolyn came into the room.

"I'll get her."

"Thanks, Sis."

Carolyn gave the baby her pacifier, and she drifted off to sleep. Carolyn stood and patted the baby's back. She glanced down and saw the action plan plotted out in her sister's notebook.

"Vanessa, what are you doing? Are you actually trying to plan out how to get a man? You can't make a man be with you."

"I have to do what's best for my baby."

"So, you think this will work? Did he say or do anything to make you think he wanted to be with you? He wasn't here for you throughout the entire pregnancy."

"He didn't know about it. He promised to be here for the baby."

"Yes, 'Nessa, for the baby."

"We are a package deal," she sang out sweetly.

Carolyn did not press the issue even though she felt as if her sister was delusional. She let her mind drift for a moment. *Brendan has grown into an attractive man,* she thought. It had been over twenty years since she'd seen him last. She couldn't let her mind go there. She didn't want to think about it. Carolyn looked over at her sister and shook her head as she walked out of the room. Vanessa continued writing out her plans.

Carolyn told her sister she needed to get home. She walked to her car and got in. She put the key in the ignition but couldn't turn the key. She sat with her head on the steering wheel and cried. The memories of that summer had haunted her for many years. She felt she could not be silent anymore.

***

After a week of diapers and four a.m. feedings, the joy of motherhood began to wane. Vanessa was not used to having her sleep disrupted, nor was she used to the demands of a newborn. Her mother returned and insisted on staying a few weeks with her new grandbaby. Having her mom there helped with her anxiety. Vanessa enviously watched her mom handle the baby. Vanessa was clumsy when feeding her and slow when changing her. Her mother could change her in half the time and feed her without making a mess. After a few days, Vanessa's mom had the baby on a schedule that everyone could live with.

Vanessa had glamorized pregnancy and motherhood so long that she forgot about all the hard work it entailed. Bottles, pacifiers, and diapers were just the beginning. She realized that financially she was not in good shape, after all. She forgot things like babysitter, daycare, pediatrician visits and the constant attention that babies need. Now that Brenda was on a schedule, it was a little better, but the first week was definitely an eye-opener.

Brendan hadn't called her since the weekend. At least, she had his contact information, so she planned to use it. He said he would be there for the baby, and she hoped he would. Taking care of a baby was definitely a two-person job.

"Well, it's about time for me to go," announced her mother a few weeks later.

"Mom, please stay. She does so much better with you here."

"Vanessa, it's time for me to go home. I have my own place and my own life. You have to learn to do this on your own."

"I know, and I will, but could you at least stay until Saturday? Please?" she asked in a whiny voice.

"Okay, Saturday it is," her mother said with a smile. *It feels good to be needed,* her mother thought as she walked towards the kitchen for a cup of tea.

Vanessa sighed with relief and took a seat in her rocker. Carolyn arrived shortly after the conversation. When she noticed how worn out Vanessa looked, she shooed her off to bed. "Go lay down. Me and Mom got this."

"Okay, thanks, sis," she said heading out of the nursery almost knocking her mom over who was returning to the room. "Mom, I didn't see you!"

"You need a nap!" she snapped.

"That is where I'm headed right now—bed!"

Her mom patted her shoulder and walked over to the rocker to sit down. She got settled in the rocking chair and picked up the remote, thinking to herself what a waste of money it was to put a television in a baby's room. "Now, why does a baby need a TV?" she asked out loud.

"Well, Momma, Vanessa can watch it in here with the baby or leave it on a music channel to put the baby to sleep."

"Yeah, I guess you're right. So, what are you thinking so hard about over there? Why have you been so quiet today?" she asked, reaching for her teacup.

Carolyn didn't respond right away. She wanted to choose her words carefully. "Mom, we need to talk." The seriousness of her tone made her mother pause mid-sip. Carolyn thought a minute more before she spoke. Then she asked, "Have you seen the baby's birth certificate?"

"No. Why?"

When Carolyn explained Vanessa's child was fathered by Brendan McNair, her mother choked on her tea.

Chapter 5

Tiffany left the courthouse in a huff. Her feet angrily hit the pavement as she stormed her way over to the car. She knew the chances of him being the father were slim, so no child support would be forthcoming. There was no sense in asking Reggie for any help. Not only was he back in jail, but he also had three other children she just found out about.

Her mom wasn't going to help her anymore. She made that clear when she dropped the kids off that morning. Slim was the only man that really took care of her. She could only blame herself. The affair with Reggie was her fault. Since high school, she'd lived off one man after another. But now, she had no choice. Tiffany had to get a job.

She drove to her mother's house to retrieve her children and return her mom's car. Her mom met her at the door with the children in tow.

"Dang, Mom, were they that bad?" she asked jokingly.

"Of course not. I just want you to ride to the store with me," she said, ushering her grandson out of the door while cradling the baby in her arms.

"I just got here. Can you give me a minute?"

"No. Put him in his car seat while I secure her."

Blowing out an exasperated breath, Tiffany complied. She kissed her son and placed him in the chair. Looking at her babies always improved her mood.

"I'll drive," said her mom. "So, how did it go?" she asked after they got into the car.

"I lost the case because he is not the father. I thought I had a chance to get something anyway because we were married when she was born, but that didn't matter."

"You had a good husband, Tiffany. You messed that up."

Tiffany sucked her teeth in response.

"Look, Tiffany, you are a grown woman. It's time to act like it. You have two children to raise. The father is a jailbird, so you have to take care of your own responsibilities."

"I know that, Momma," Tiffany snapped.

"Get smart again," her mom warned. "Don't forget who you are talking to. I am still your mother. The hotel on the corner is hiring all positions, and a lot of them don't require experience."

"Okay, fine. I'll check it out tomorrow," Tiffany replied and turned her head.

"No, ma'am. You will check it out today. As a matter of fact, we are headed there now," stated her mom in a firm voice.

Tiffany wanted to protest but knew it was useless. Besides, her mom was right. She really needed a job. The baby was low on pampers already. The little money she had would only last a few days. She took a deep breath and exhaled. She brought this on herself. Reggie was only good for one thing. That one thing left her with two kids, and she had to feed them.

They pulled up to the hotel and parked. Tiffany walked in to grab an application and turned to go. The lady at the desk explained that if she waited she could interview shortly. Tiffany almost said no but decided to try her luck. She ran out and told her mom to give her a few minutes. After she finished the application, she was sent into a room to interview.

The executive housekeeper told her she had an immediate opening in the laundry room and would like to offer her the job contingent upon a background check. Tiffany eagerly accepted the position. She wanted a desk job but knew she'd better take anything she could get for now. It didn't sound so bad anyway. She would have rotating weekends off and paid training. The position also offered medical benefits. Tiffany smiled despite herself.

***

Slim felt like a weight had been lifted off his shoulders. He walked out of the courtroom whistling.

Since he had the rest of the day off, he decided to go to his mom's house. Remembering Joy was off, he called to see if she wanted to come along.

Slim knew things were shaky with Joy. He truly loved her and wanted her to be his wife. He didn't want to lose her. After watching his daughter come into the world, his entire way of thinking changed. He had to figure out how to maintain his relationship with Joy and co-parent with Vanessa. He did not foresee this as being a comfortable situation, but he would do the best he could.

Seeing Joy walk out the door made his heart swell. When Joy saw the smile on his face, she too felt relieved. She had grabbed a few snacks for them to take on the ride. He reached out and took the bag from her and gave her a smack on the lips.

Slim told her on the phone that it was over and that he wasn't the father of Tiffany's daughter, but Joy wanted details. "So, how did she take it?" she asked.

"She was mad enough to chew nails," he answered shaking his head. "She kept trying to say that legally I should be responsible because I was her husband when the child was born. That girl is always trying to get something for nothing."

"Well, I, for one, am glad that is over."

"Make that two," he said, causing them both to laugh.

"Did you get any info about the other baby?" Joy asked.

Slim shook his head yes but didn't speak right away. He reached over, grabbed her hand and said, "The test proves that she is my daughter."

"Okay, so how are you going to deal with that timewise? You told me that she lives over a hundred miles away."

"Honestly, I don't know. She and I have not talked about it."

"Oh."

Slim squeezed her hand.

"Look, I don't want you to feel like this has to be a problem. You are who I want and need. I plan to have a relationship with my daughter. I can't change who her mother is. I don't love her mother; I love you. I know this is a lot to accept. But please understand I am in this relationship with you for the duration."

"Okay," she said and gave him her best fake smile. She wasn't happy about the situation, but she did appreciate the fact that he was upfront with her. There was nothing she could do about it. Joy kept up with the small talk until they arrived at Slim's mother's house.

When he pulled up, he walked around to the passenger's side to open the door for his lady. He gave her a reassuring hug and kiss before starting towards the house. His mother was overjoyed at the surprise visit. She soon had a lunch fit for a king on the table.

"Dig in, guys!"

"Thanks, Momma," said Slim as he loaded his plate with the delicious offerings. Claire was pleased to see that Joy didn't act shy either. Joy watched the interaction between mother and son. Their bond was strong. She didn't know she was smiling until his mother asked her about it.

"What are you grinning about, girl?" asked his mother.

"You two, it's refreshing to see a close relationship like this."

"Well, we only have each other," said Slim as he refilled his glass with iced tea.

"Dessert anyone? I have ice cream and cake," said his mother. "There are a few pieces of mail here for you, son." She stood and handed him a small stack of envelopes.

Slim laid the mail on the table, and one letter caught his attention.

"Man, I forgot about this!"

"What is it, Son?"

"The 401K plan. I used your address. Remember all that trouble I had with the mail at my old apartment before I married Tiffany. I was so used to the money coming out of my check that I forgot." Slim excitedly opened the letter. "Woo-wee, I got close to thirty grand!" He walked over to his mom and kissed her on the cheek. "I'm gonna buy you something nice, Momma!"

"I'm fine; you need to keep it for that new baby," she said then instantly regretted it. She looked worriedly over at Joy. She didn't know if he'd told her about the baby yet.

"She knows, Mom. There are no secrets between us. This lady right here is going to be my wife soon." His declaration made his intentions clear.

Joy now had a genuine smile on her face, and so did his mother.

Chapter 6

Vanessa made inquiries and found that a teaching position was available a few miles outside of Slim's town. Things were falling into place just like she planned. She hated to leave her house, but some things were more important. She knew the distance between them would be a hindrance, so moving was her only option. Vanessa did not want any impediments in the way of her getting her man.

She applied online and was scheduled to interview in a week. She planned to drive up the day after her six-week checkup. Her mother agreed to watch the baby after Carolyn declined. She didn't know why Carolyn was acting so difficult. *Maybe she's jealous,* she thought, but she had her husband, and Vanessa was determined to get hers.

Vanessa felt that moving would be a good thing. Brendan needed to be a part of the baby's life, which was hard to do a hundred miles away. Her daughter deserved to have both parents present in her life. Vanessa planned to secure a position then find an apartment. She had already checked around and found a hotel that offered weekly rates. She felt she could deal with a hotel until a suitable apartment became available.

She had a good feeling about the interview. After the interview, she stopped at a gas station to refuel and pick up an apartment guide. Apartment living didn't sound all that appealing, but she felt it would be only temporary. At first, she looked into renting a house, but they were too expensive. After driving through several apartment complexes, she decided two of them looked promising. She stopped in to pick up information brochures and chatted with the rental agents.

The time went quickly, and it would soon be dark. She decided to stay overnight. She reached out to her mother to let her know about the change in plans. After purchasing toiletries and other essentials, she checked into a hotel and ordered takeout.

The next morning, she made several calls to get information on apartments, U-Haul rental, and movers. Once she'd added up the estimated cost, she realized the enormity of her decision. To move would be very expensive. Another thing she had to consider was the baby. If she moved, she would have to depend upon strangers to keep her. Was that really what she wanted to do?

She made several inquiries and found that daycare for infants was almost as much as rent. Maybe moving there wasn't a good idea, after all. She knew it would be a huge change for her, and Brendan hadn't given her any sign of changing his mind yet. He called and checked on the baby but hadn't been back to see her because of his schedule. She decided to table her decision to move until she had a better relationship with him. She gathered her things, packed her car, and headed to the lobby to check out.

***

Tiffany thanked her friend for the ride and walked into the lobby of the hotel. Her shift started at noon, so she had time to kill. She took a seat in the lobby to wait.

"Tiffany, you can clock in now and just leave a little early if you want," said her supervisor who was on her way to the snack machine.

"Thanks."

"Oh yeah, don't let me forget to give you your uniforms before you leave; they came in today."

"Thanks, I won't," Tiffany replied and walked over to the front counter to enter in her clock-in code.

A dark-skinned female approached the desk obviously wanting to check out. Thinking that she was being ignored, the guest began rapidly tapping her keycard on the counter. "Excuse me," said the guest.

Tiffany was so engrossed in what she was doing that she didn't hear her.

"I need to check out and get my receipt," the guest said louder.

Tiffany looked up and was about to go off but stopped and stated, "I'm sorry, I'll get someone for you."

The on-duty clerk and Joy were in the back breakroom and heard the guest. The clerk came out to assist the guest, and Joy walked over to assist Tiffany.

"Oh, ma'am, I am sorry. I did not see you on the monitor. You were out of camera range. How can I help you?" the clerk asked.

Joy busied herself by assisting Tiffany with her ID card.

"You must be new?" asked Joy.

"Yes, I'm in laundry," replied Tiffany.

The guest overheard the exchange and apologized for her blunder. All of the ladies looked up as Slim walked into the door. Joy smiled when she saw him, but the look on his face caused her to raise an eyebrow.

"Brendan, what's wrong?" she asked walking towards him.

Before he could respond, Tiffany spoke. "How do you know my husband?"

"Ex-husband," corrected Slim.

Tiffany decided not to push her luck and was about to leave when the guest spoke up. "Hello, Brendan, fancy meeting you here."

Not wanting to miss anything, Tiffany stopped and stared blatantly eavesdropping.

"Hello," he said and then looked at Joy. "This is Vanessa." He faced Vanessa and said, "Vanessa, this is Joy, my fiancée."

Joy heard the hard edge in his voice and knew why he introduced her as his fiancée. He had told her about the way Vanessa was trying to push him into a relationship. After giving birth, she was even more persistent.

"Well, I be damned," said Tiffany, finding the situation hilarious. "Who are you then?" she asked Vanessa.

"I'm the real mother of his child," Vanessa said with attitude.

After being put in her place, Tiffany stopped laughing, turned, and walked away in a huff.

"What brings you here, Vanessa? Is the baby alright?" Slim asked.

"She is fine. I just had some business to tend to."

Slim didn't believe her for a minute but didn't press her. Frankly, he didn't care.

"Well, Joy and I have a lunch date." He put his arm around Joy's waist.

Joy told the wide-eyed clerk she would be back in an hour. In the car, Brendan reached over and grabbed her hand. "Wow," she said.

"Yeah, I didn't want you all to meet like that."

"We had to meet sooner or later."

"Tiffany works here?"

"Yeah, she works in laundry. I didn't know she was your ex. I didn't hire her."

"I can't believe she got a job. I hope she doesn't cause a problem. I know it must feel strange knowing you are working with my ex-wife."

"Look, I come in before most of the staff and leave after them. I barely see anyone other than the front desk. Besides, I'm not about petty drama. You two are divorced. She won't be a problem."

"Good. So, are we okay?"

"Yes, we are fine," she said with a small smile.

She knew he had a past, and so did she. There was no reason to be concerned yet. However, like Slim, she wondered what business Vanessa had in town.

***

Furious, Vanessa stormed out of the hotel. *His fiancée? Why didn't he ever say anything about her?* How dare he humiliate her like that? Reality hit her hard. He never said he was going to marry her. She thought having his baby would change his mind about her. Vanessa had to come to grips with the fact that he did not love her. He was in love with someone else.

She'd lost hope of having him before she realized she was pregnant. She thought being pregnant would increase her chances. Having him at the birth gave her even more reason to believe she had a chance. *Well, I'm glad I didn't get any further in my plans,* she thought bitterly.

Carolyn was right. He was only concerned about Brenda. Well, he would have a hard time seeing her. She vowed to make it hard for him. Tears came fast and heavy. Trying to compose herself, she took several deep breaths. She called her mom to let her know she was on the way back, but Vanessa never made it. In her emotional state, she didn't see the eighteen-wheeler until it was too late.

***

Reggie stood outside waiting for his ride. He had been released early due to a technicality. He had called one of his buddies to get a ride home. They pulled up to Tiffany's apartment and rang the bell. When she didn't answer, he went next door to the lady who sometimes babysat for her. She came to the door and told him Tiffany was at work. Once he got over his initial shock, he asked her if she knew where. Then, he persuaded his friend to take him to the hotel to get a key.

The men pulled up to the front entrance, and Reggie jumped out. He looked back at his friend and yelled, "Hey, while I go get the key, run around the corner and get some beers. We can chill at her crib for a while."

"Bet."

Reggie walked in and stood in line until it was his turn.

"Um, can you tell me where to find Tiffany?" he asked the clerk when it was finally his turn.

"I can have her meet you here," replied the clerk.

"Thanks." He took a seat, looking around at people as they walked by.

The desk called to the laundry room and told Tiffany she had a visitor. When she got up front and saw it was Reggie, she turned around to walk away.

"Hey! Where are you going?"

"I thought you were locked up."

"Look, I just need the key."

"What key?"

"To the apartment."

"You want the key to *my* house? Are you crazy? Do you really think I'm gonna let you lay up in my house while I am out here working to feed your children? Get lost, Reggie." She turned to walk away, and he grabbed her arm. She looked at him and asked, "So, you must be ready to go back to jail? Why don't you go stay with your other baby momma? I hear that you got quite a few to choose from."

Realizing she had the upper hand at the moment, he let her go and walked out. He would have to find other accommodations for the night. Maybe his wife would be more receptive.

***

Brendan pulled up to the hotel to bring Joy back from lunch.

"Well, I'll be damn. Look who it is," he said seeing Reggie walk out the door.

"Who is he?"

"The real father of Tiffany's kids."

"Oh Lord, what kind of day is this?"

Brendan was about to speak when his cell rang. The caller ID showed that it was the hospital.

"Hello."

"I am calling from G-E-N Hospital. We have a patient here that we believe to be your wife."

"What?"

"Vanessa Plumber is on her ID. Your number is on her phone as Husband."

"Is she okay?" he asked, not bothering to correct her.

"She was in an accident and is currently in surgery."

"I'm on my way," he said as he threw down the phone.

"Vanessa had a wreck. I need to go to the hospital," he said to Joy once he disconnected the call.

"Okay, keep me posted."

Brendan knew as long as the hospital thought he was her husband he could get the information he needed. It only took ten minutes to get to the hospital and park his car.

The doctor told him she was still unconscious. He stated that her vitals were good, but he was concerned about her head injury. Brendan thanked the doctor for the information and started to leave. Then, it dawned on him that her mother and the rest of her family probably didn't know she had been in an accident.

"Excuse me. Where is her cell?"

The nurse handed him a bag with her purse, phone, and other personal items. Brendan took on the job of calling her family.

***

When Joy got home, she walked straight to the bedroom to unwind. She ran a bath and dropped in her favorite scented bubble bath. She had just started to relax when her doorbell rang. She slipped on her robe and went to the door. Seeing Brendan, she hurriedly opened the door.

"Hey baby, how is she?"

"Unconscious."

"Will she make it?"

"Don't know, the doc is concerned about her head injury."

"Oh my goodness! What about the baby?"

"She is with Vanessa's mother. The hospital released her cell phone to me, and I called them."

She reached up and hugged him. Without words, she walked him down the hall to the bathroom and helped him undress.

"Get in the tub and soak," she ordered.

Brendan complied without a word. She gave him a massage and told him it would all work out. After the bath, the couple ate a light supper and called it a night. The couple settled in and tried to sleep. Brendan thought about all the things that transpired the last few months and prayed things worked out. He was in a complicated situation. The only thing that made life bearable was Joy. He was going to need her more than he realized.

Sometime during the night, he awakened feeling a strong desire to hold Joy closer to him. He cradled Joy in his arms and held onto her as if he never wanted to lose her. Moving her also woke her. She turned and faced him. He reached down and took her hand and removed her blocker.

"Let me replace this ring. Marry me. I meant what I said at my mom's house. I have been through hell and high water, and you stayed right with me. I need you in my life. I don't want to rush you, but I do want you to know that I'm for real. I would have asked you sooner, but I didn't want to scare you off. But now, I know you don't scare easily. With all that has been going on, anyone else would have left me by now."

"Brendan."

"Let me finish. When I married Tiffany, it was more out of obligation. Once we divorced, I realized I wanted a family. I was really hurt because of the loss of my son. I still want a family, and I want it with you. I'm too old to waste five years of my life being engaged. Be my wife. Don't say no," he said as he kissed her tenderly. That kiss led to another and another. "Say yes," he whispered against her neck.

Joy was too caught up in the moment to speak. Brendan wasn't playing fair. He wanted to take his time convincing her to say yes. But she had to put a stop to his plans.

"I have to go to work. I have a meeting. I'm not saying no, but I still want you to convince me to say yes later on."

He smiled and replied, "All night long."

"A lifetime," she shot back and jumped out of bed.

He followed her to the bathroom with plans of a quickie in the shower. They showered, dressed and headed towards the front door.

"I'm going to stop by the hospital on my way to work," he said.

"Okay," she answered. "But take this."

"What?"

"Your key."

Brendan felt the happiest he'd felt in a long time.

***

Slim pulled into the hospital's parking lot and let out a long sigh. He lit a cigarette and took a long pull. He wasn't ready to face her family, but he was sure they would be there by now. He still had trouble with the fact that Carolyn was Vanessa's sister. Seeing Carolyn again brought back a myriad of conflicting feelings. He wasn't sure how to handle the situation.

He dropped the cigarette in the ashtray outside of the hospital and walked inside. He walked to the room and found it empty. Thinking she was moved to another room, he went to the nurse's station to find out where. When he got there, he found Vanessa's mother talking with the doctor. Carolyn was sitting in one of the chairs. When she saw him, she stood, walked over to him, and fell into his arms. He did not refuse her. He held her and rubbed her back. She held her head up and looked at him.

"Vanessa didn't make it. She died," she told him.

In shock, he held onto Carolyn as she silently wept. Carolyn broke the embrace and walked over to the baby who had started crying. The baby would not take her bottle or be consoled. Brendan gently took the baby from her, and she immediately stopped crying. He smiled at his precious child. He propped her up on his shoulder and started walking.

"Where do you think you're going with that baby? Put her down!" Vanessa's mother yelled.

"What?"

"You put that baby down!"

"This is my daughter," Slim's menacing voice startled her for a moment.

She lowered her voice and said, "You took my daughter away from me. You did this! She was here to see you."

"I didn't even know she was here. I happened to see her checking out of the hotel where my fiancée works."

Carolyn interrupted, "Momma, we are all hurting here, but you can't blame him for this. 'Nessa came up here because she was trying to move here. He probably didn't even know."

"She what?" he asked incredulously.

"She was planning on moving here. She had a job interview the other day," Carolyn explained.

"She never said anything to me about it," he said.

"Either way, he is the reason she was here. *Him!* You ruined both my girls. Give me my grandbaby!" Vanessa's mother yelled, reaching for the child.

"No." The finality in his voice stopped her in her tracks. He did not yell, but his voice meant business.

Vanessa's mother heard the steel in his voice and backed away a few feet before saying, "You can't have another one of my girls."

"She is my daughter, and you will not come between us."

"Please don't do this here," interrupted the nurse. "I know this is a shock, but please let's calm down," she looked pleadingly at them.

Slim was the first to speak. "Mrs. Plummer, Vanessa just died. We are all in shock and emotional, but understand this one thing, this is my child. Mine."

Carolyn sat silently crying, and her mother suddenly turned her wrath on her.

"And how could you defend him after all he did to you?"

"Not now Momma, 'Nessa just died. My sister is gone. She was in an accident. It was no one's fault. Just Stop! Stop! STOP!"

Her mother plopped in a nearby chair and began to sob.

Brendan left his contact information with Carolyn telling her to contact him about the funeral. He picked up the child's car seat and diaper bag and walked out of the hospital.

***

Joy sat in the conference room waiting. The meeting was to start shortly. The clerk on duty brought in pastries and beverages for the meeting. The two ladies were busy setting up when Brendan came through the door with a baby in his arms. His distress was evident, so she rushed over to him.

"Come on to my office. What's wrong?"

"She died. Vanessa is gone."

"What? Okay, look I need you to wait here. I will be back as soon as possible. Please," said Joy.

"Okay."

She took a look down at the small brown face in his arms then back up at him. "It will be okay."

Joy walked back into the conference room and sat down. Before she could get herself together, the corporate agents came through the door. She pasted on her fake smile and extended her hand to the agent she was acquainted with.

"Good morning, Chris. Good morning, gentleman," she began. She was familiar with Chris but not the other two men. She had assumed it would be a routine meeting, but seeing two unfamiliar agents, she felt a bit apprehensive.

They each returned the greeting and took a seat.

"Let's get down to business," said Chad.

Joy smiled and waited.

"You have been running this place for months with all the time off your GM has been taking. We have been watching you. You have shown yourself capable. We are here to offer you the general manager position. Mrs. Parker will not be returning."

After a few seconds of tense silence, Joy smiled and extended her hand.

"I accept."

Chad shook her hand and started going over her new contract. Afterward, Joy's face hurt from smiling so long. The enormous jump in pay was more than generous. She started clearing the table when she suddenly remembered Brendan was still waiting in her office.

Joy hurried to her office and found them both fast asleep. Brendan was sitting in her chair holding the baby.

"Brendan," she gently shook his shoulder. His eyes were heavy with sleep and grief. "Honey, are you okay?"

"Yeah," he said as he readjusted the baby in his arms

"Tell me what happened."

"She died sometime last night."

"Oh my goodness! How did you end up with the baby?"

"I picked her up because she was crying and started walking around to calm her, and Mrs. Plummer just lost it. She didn't want me to have my own child."

"Okay, so how are we going to take care of her?"

"We will have to figure it out," he said with a hopeful look on his face.

"Yeah, we will," she said and smiled, but a few days later she was ready to call it quits. The house was a mess. Brendan stayed at her house more often than not. The baby cried all the time, and they were never able to just relax.

When she pulled into her driveway that afternoon, she sat in the car for a few minutes. It was never agreed on, but it looked like Brendan and Brenda were moving in. Well, ground rules would have to be set. She was already tired of a messy house and smelly diapers. Most new moms have at least nine months to prepare. She had one day.

When she opened the front door, she was pleasantly surprised. The house was spotless. No baby toys or bottles were lying about. The only thing she could smell was dinner and cleaning products. He must have felt she was not too happy with the way things had been going lately. The house was quiet for a change. She found Brendan asleep in the bed with the baby lying close by. The sight of them changed everything in that instant. She had a family.

While they slept, she sketched out a plan for one of the larger bedrooms. Now that she had a little girl, she wanted her to have her own room. She smiled as she planned out the room. A child does change things. She wasn't expecting her, but she was beginning to love her.

Tonya

***

Reggie knew that his wife would be at work. He also knew she never locked the back bedroom window. He crawled through and took his time looking for any signs of another man. Not finding any, he took a shower and put on some clean clothes. He was actually surprised he still had clothes there. He rummaged through the cabinets for food. After helping himself, he plopped down on the sofa and promptly fell asleep.

Her key in the front door woke him. He sat up and greeted her.

"Hey, baby, daddy's home."

The look on her face let him know she did not want to see him.

"What are you doing here? Let me guess, she put you out?"

"Gee Gee, I'm here 'cause I want to be. Where are my sons?"

"None of your business. Why are you in my house, Reginald?"

"Our house. I'm still your husband, remember?"

"Do you remember I haven't seen you in months?" Gee asked.

"I was in jail, Gee."

"Reginald, I don't—"

"Gee-Gee, I was in jail. You can ask Po-Boy. He brought me home, and you can verify with the jail."

"Why didn't you call or write then?

"It was the day after we had a fight. I didn't think you would answer."

She knew he was lying. His wife knew precisely when he went to jail and where he was before going. She didn't call him on his lie. Since they had been together, he'd been in jail for petty crimes. Fighting, driving without a license, public intoxication and other nonsense. She knew about the other women and other children. She didn't call him on this but said, "You can sleep on the sofa tonight, but you have to go in the morning."

"I'll stay as long as I want. I'm your husband, and you can't put me out."

"All you have to do is sign the papers, and you won't be."

"Fine. If that is the way you want it, I will."

Reggie didn't want to go back to jail. If they got into it again, all she had to do was call the cops. He realized he could not charm her anymore. Knowing his options were limited, he had to secure a place to stay. Tiffany was a no go, and his other lady friend had got married and moved away, taking his daughter with her.

Damn. Trying to be a 'player' was not working out for him. He only married Gee-Gee because she got pregnant. He thought he was doing the right thing. After the newness of marriage wore off, he started up with Keisha and later Tiffany. Now, he had three outside kids plus the two with his wife. In a few years, he would be thirty. Jail and babies were all he had accomplished.

He decided to play it cool. He sat on the sofa and channel surfed. His wife made lunch for herself then left to finish her shift. He called his friend for a ride. He decided he was going to try Tiffany one more time.

***

Vanessa's death forced Brendan to put things into perspective. He had to acknowledge the fact that his life could end at any time. He also had to be there for his daughter. Joy was so far beyond understanding. He felt she was overwhelmed with his intrusion. He wanted to make things right with her. Lately, he was more attentive and made sure he took on some of the household chores. The transition was hard for both of them, but he was grateful to have her and his mother in his corner. He knew he could not raise Brenda alone.

A few days after Vanessa's death Brendan received a phone call from Carolyn.

"Brendan, the funeral will be Saturday."

"I'll be there. Do you need anything?" he asked.

"No."

"Are you sure, Carolyn?"

"Yeah, I'm sure. Vanessa was a planner. She had everything arranged and paid for."

"Okay, so what time and where?" Brendan asked.

Carolyn gave him the time and directions

"Thank you, Carolyn. I hate that we had to meet again under these circumstances."

"Yeah, it has been a long time."

"See you Saturday," he said.

"See you Saturday."

Brendan felt she wanted to say more, but he wasn't in the mood to dredge up the past. They were torn apart as teenagers and never had a chance to say goodbye. He never imagined he would see her again. It took a long time to get over it, but their time was over. Over twenty years had passed, and he was well over the heartbreak.

Brendan insisted on Joy attending the funeral with him. He felt uneasy about dealing with Vanessa's family. He knew her mother was going to be a problem. She was obviously still upset about the summer he and Carolyn were together, as well. The more he thought about it, the more he didn't want to go. Joy was aware of his misgivings but pressed upon him the importance of going and paying his last respects. She also felt it would give him closure.

They started out very early that morning dropping the baby off at his mother's house for the weekend. He really appreciated his mother's help. He didn't want a tug of war with his child, so he felt it best that she stay at home.

Once they arrived in town, they stopped at a gas station to refuel and freshen up. He noticed a young woman that had a striking resemblance to Carolyn. *She must be here for the funeral*, he thought to himself. Joy was busy gathering snacks and hadn't noticed the female. Brendan was intrigued. The young lady looked like a young Carolyn with a slightly darker complexion. The memories of that summer came flooding back to him. He wanted to ask her name, but Joy distracted him.

"Hon, do you want a soda?"

"Yeah a Coke," he turned to respond and when he turned back around the young lady was gone.

"Are you okay?" Joy asked.

"Yeah, I'm fine." He paid for their snacks and headed to the car.

Deep in thought, Brendan drove to the funeral. Joy respected his silence. The town was not very big. Therefore, finding the church wasn't hard. They parked and entered the building, taking a seat at the back. He scanned the funeral program and realized that even though they had a child together, he didn't know her. He thought about his daughter and the questions she would have later on. What would he tell her when she asked about her mother?

He decided against going to the gravesite after her mother made it known that she didn't want him there. She was very vocal at the church, and since he didn't want to cause a scene, he left without a word.

Carolyn made eye contact and nodded. She desperately wanted to talk to him but knew now was not the time. She silently watched Brendan walk away.

Chapter 7

A Saturday off was just what Joy needed. She wanted to sleep late, but the baby didn't agree with that. She headed to the kitchen to fix her a bottle and then call Portia. She really didn't feel like doing anything but resting. Since being promoted and the added responsibilities at home, she needed a rest. She looked down at the little brown face and smiled. She walked and bounced her, hoping she would go back to sleep. The wedding planning would have to wait. There was just too much going on right now.

Portia grabbed the fabric swatches, books, magazines, and tulle. Planning the wedding was more work than she anticipated. Although she was having a small wedding, she still wanted it done right. After she found a seamstress, she had to get the material and sewing notions. Joy was supposed to help her with the work. After she loaded her car, she headed to Joy's house. Planning the wedding was exciting at first, but now it felt like work.

She drove the few miles to Joy's house and ran up the walk. After a few knocks, Joy came to the door with a baby in her arms.

"Who's baby is that?" she asked, walking into the house.

"Come on in, Portia," Joy said walking towards the kitchen completely ignoring her question. "As you can see, I'm busy. I just don't have time today."

"Well, when then? I only have a few weeks. You said you would help me," Portia whined.

"This child's mother just died, and her father is trying to sleep."

"Oh, I'm sorry. I didn't mean to sound selfish," Portia said sincerely.

"I'm sorry. I should not have snapped. You didn't know. She will be sleeping soon, and I will try to carve out an hour for you, okay?"

After she got the baby down for a nap, she had Portia make out a list of things she needed and wanted to be done. She took the list and divided it up amongst her friends that had agreed to help. She suggested they meet again in a week to see what everyone had accomplished. Portia loved the idea. It would not overload any one person, and the work would be done quickly.

"Thank you, Joy. Your organizational skills are second to none. It would have taken me weeks to get this planned and organized," said Portia.

"You're welcome, girl," Joy said as Brenda woke from her nap demanding to be fed and be changed. "Well, duty calls. I'll see you next week."

"Thanks again, Joy! I don't know what I'd do without you."

Joy smiled and walked Portia to the door. She picked up the baby and held her close; the sweet baby smell was intoxicating. Joy looked down at the baby in her arms and said, "What have I gotten myself into?"

Monday morning, Joy put the stressful weekend behind her and got busy relocating to the General Manager's office. She was rearranging the furniture when Tristan walked in.

"Hi there, stranger," he said, getting her attention.

"Tristan, how are you?"

"What's going on in here?" he asked as he looked around the office.

"I got promoted, so I'm moving on up." She handed him a box, and he followed her out of the door.

"When did all this happen?" Tristan asked.

"It all happened a few days ago. So, what brings you by?" she asked, taking a seat at her new desk.

"I haven't seen you in weeks, and the last time I saw you things were not that great."

"I'm fine." Just got a lot on my plate right now, but I'm fine."

Knowing her as well as he did, he knew she wasn't telling the truth or, at least, the entire truth. He stared at her for a few seconds then walked over to a nearby chair and sat down. "Okay, I'm listening."

"It turns out that a past fling got pregnant. She had a baby."

"Whoa! So now what are you going to do? I mean, are you ready to deal with baby Momma drama?" he asked.

"We will have to deal with it."

"We? Why do you have to deal with it? Don't you think that is a bit much?" Tristan asked.

"He and I are together Tristan, and we will deal with it." The finality in Joy's voice was not missed. Tristan rose and took his queue.

"I'll check on you later."

Joy wasn't sure how much she wanted to reveal to Tristan. She didn't even tell him the mother had passed away. She had shared so much with him over the years, but she didn't want to share this. She was struggling with the situation and wanted to make up her own mind about it.

Unloading all her issues may take some of the pressure off, but then again, the things she needed to say should be said to Brendan. She was in love with Brendan, but it was a great deal of work to care for a new baby. She felt like the situation could rapidly get out of hand. However, Tristan was not the person to talk to about it.

***

Brendan drove home with a small bag on the passenger seat. He opened the door to a clean house and dinner. The baby was lying in her bassinet happily waving her arms. She was fascinated with the recently purchased mobile spinning over her head. He and Joy had purchased quite a few things for the baby recently. He was grateful for her contributions. The baby literally had two changes of clothes when he brought her home.

He found Joy in the kitchen preparing dinner. Joy had her back to him and was clearing the counter. He felt at home, and he wanted to make it permanent.

"Ahem."

Joy didn't turn around, so he walked over to her and tapped her shoulder before slowly kneeling. She turned and looked down at the opened burgundy ring box. Her birthstone surrounded by diamonds stared back at her. Teary-eyed, she dropped the sponge, pulled out her ear-buds, and grabbed the box. Brendan stood and kissed her deeply. She held him and poured everything into the kiss.

"Have I convinced you to say yes, yet?"

"Maybe," she said with a playful smile.

***

The following Saturday Portia reached out to everyone working on the wedding and was happy to find out that most of the work was done. She had just finished her final fitting and headed to Joy's house. Joy came to the door in shorts and a tee shirt. Her hair was a mess, and she had stains on her shirt. Despite all of that, she looked blissfully happy—a fact Portia failed to notice.

"Wow!" Portia said, looking around the room and noticing the toys and loads of laundry on the sofa.

"Oh, hi girl. Come on in," said Joy.

"You look, hmmm, well different."

Joy smiled and said, "Well, the baby is a handful. Excuse me a moment." She returned with a clean tee shirt and was busy pulling her hair into a ponytail.

Portia noticed the new shiny ring but didn't mention it.

"Better?" Joy asked.

Portia was busy looking around. "Joy, are they living here?"

"Why do you ask?" she asked, putting her hands on her hips.

Feeling the change in her attitude, Portia let it drop. "Nothing, never mind. Look, the list is almost done. The only thing I have to do is order the groom cake, and we are done. Your fitting is Wednesday, and the wedding rehearsal is Friday."

Joy was only half listening. She was busy sorting and folding the laundry.

"You are not listening!" Portia suddenly shouted.

"Portia, I have a lot to do. I hear you, but your wedding is not my top priority right now. As you can see, I have things to do." Joy spread her hand out to illustrate.

"One of the things should be to get a maid. I have never seen your house this messy," Portia retorted.

"Well, you can leave, Portia," Joy snapped.

"What about the wedding, Joy?"

"What about it?" Joy glared at her.

Portia grabbed her purse and stormed out. Before she was backed out of the driveway, she had Joy's mother on the phone.

Joy was putting up the last of the laundry when the phone rang. Her mother demanded to know why a man and his child were living with her.

"Mother, I am well over twenty-one. Please let me live my life."

"I know your age, and don't forget who you are talking to," her mother angrily replied.

"Mother, I am a grown woman. I don't need your permission to do anything."

"I'm calling out of concern, Jocelyn. I don't want to see you hurt again."

"Okay, Mother. I'm sorry; I didn't mean to be disrespectful," Joy said in a lighter tone.

"You didn't even tell me that you were engaged. I had to hear that from Portia. She said you were wearing a new ring."

"Mother, it just happened. I have not told anyone yet. Portia just guessed."

"Were you going to tell me?" her mother asked.

Joy sighed. "Of course, I was going to tell you."

"Well, I had to find out about your divorce from other people," her mother started.

"I have to go, Mom."

"Jocelyn, don't you dare hang up this phone. I'm talking to you."

Joy disconnected the call and unplugged the phone. She finished her housework and checked on the baby. Her mother may have meant well, but she did not need any more advice. After a day or so, she would call her back and apologize but not today.

Joy felt terrible about the blow up with Portia. So the next day to make amends, she called and invited her to lunch. The ladies met at their favorite Chinese restaurant. Portia was her oldest friend. However, she could be a bit shallow at times. Portia arrived late as usual. She walked in looking like a runway model. Joy shook her head at her antics. Portia always felt more secure if she thought she was the best looking woman in the room, even when it was only her opinion. Portia thought she had 'come up in the world' since she was dating a wealthy banker. The man looked to be at least twenty years older than her. Joy never said anything to Portia, but he made her feel uneasy.

"Hi, thanks for coming," Joy said.

"Hello." Portia's tone was distant.

"Portia, I'm sorry. I know you have a lot to deal with right now, but so do I. And just like I am here for you, I need you to understand that I have things to deal with as well. And I know that you are concerned."

"Well, yeah, I'm very concerned. I mean, he is beneath you. He is a blue-collar plant worker. Why would you marry him? What does he have to offer?" Joy bit the inside of her lip. Portia continued with, "…and he comes with baggage. If a man I'm with has baggage, then they need to be filled with money."

"Really, Portia?"

"Look, you are well educated. You come from a good family. I bet he lives in a little apartment, drives an old car, and was probably raised by a teenage mother. What could he really offer you?" Portia continued with her rant as she scanned the menu.

Joy considered her to be a friend, but as she listened to her, she realized she was not the type of person she needed in her life, especially now.

"Portia, did I ever say anything negative to you about your fiancée?"

"What is there to say?" Portia asked with a flip of her newly purchased hair. "He is rich and takes good care of me. I'm moving to a huge house, I'll have—"

"Stop." Joy calmly placed her menu on the table and gathered her things. "This conversation is over. There is no need to continue. You wouldn't understand the concept of marrying for love."

"What do you mean? I love—"

"Portia, you are marrying an old, rich white man for his money. You love the money and the things that come with them. I get that you never had anything, so I understand why you are with him. I never judged you. I was your friend. I tried to help you plan the wedding. I was supportive. I respected your decision. But you know what? Portia, you are beneath me. I hope you enjoy your life, and I hope he enjoys the cow he bought."

Joy stood, put on her shades, and sashayed away. She was close to the hotel, so she decided to pop in and knock off a few reports and get the weekend deposits ready. She rarely worked on Sunday, but not having an assistant, she used every opportunity to get and stay ahead. Joy arrived at work in a good mood, despite the argument with Portia. She had to admit that not having to deal with the wedding decreased her stress level tremendously.

She smoothly slid her car into a parking place and headed to the front door. She planned to finish a few reports, check her emails, and call it a day. Since Portia ruined lunch, she went to the vending machine to grab a few snacks until later. She turned the corner and came face to face with her mother.

"Mom!"

"Yes, it is I, your mother. I went to your house, but your car was gone. I was just in your office, and it was empty."

"Follow me, Mom."

Joy escorted her mother to the new office. Her mother stood in the doorway and admired the large office space. She slowly turned her head to take it all in.

"Wow, so looks like you got a promotion."

"Yes, ma'am."

"Do you have any more secrets? Are you pregnant?"

"Mother, please stop. I am on my job. Do you need a room? Why are you here?"

"I came to see about you."

"I'm trying to finish up a few things and go home," Joy responded with a flip of her hair.

Suddenly noticing the difference in Joy's appearance, she asked, "So, when did you start wearing your hair loose? You look different."

"What?"

"I came because I was concerned, but it looks like I don't have to be."

"What do you mean?"

"When you divorced Morris, I think you lost a part of yourself. But, now it looks like you got it back. You look happy."

"Mom, I told you I'm doing fine."

"Well, I had to see for myself. I know that you are well over twenty-one, but you are still my baby."

"Oh, Mom," she said as her mom embraced her.

"Now, hurry up so we can go to your house. I want to meet my new grandbaby."

"Okay," Joy said with a smile.

Her mother didn't voice her true feelings. Therefore, the visit turned out to be a great one. Her mother doted on the baby and insisted on helping with the wedding when the time came. Seeing her daughter happy again was a great relief. Now, she was a new mom. It was not the conventional way, but either way, she had a grandbaby to spoil.

***

Since the baby had been enrolled into daycare, the couple fell into a weekly routine. Brendan was thrilled with his role as a father. Joy was supportive and even planned to have one of the bedrooms converted into a nursery. Slim still had a few months before his lease was up, but he rarely spent much time at his apartment. His nights were spent with Joy. The move had been gradual. Neither of them had verbalized anything. Joy had accepted him and his child without a word of protest. He didn't want to crowd her or run her off, but he needed her more than anything right now.

Mornings, Joy normally dropped the baby off at daycare, and he picked her up. Slim had enough time to run by his apartment and check the mail and check on the apartment before work. He didn't find anything out of order, so he grabbed his mail and headed out. Before he had a chance to get in his car, he was approached by a deputy sheriff.

"Are you Brendan McNair?"

"Yes, what is this about?

"Summons," the deputy sheriff said and handed him the paperwork

Brendan looked down at the paperwork

"Damn. I don't believe this!"

Now livid, he drove to work at top speed. He had to force himself to calm down. Throughout the day, he would think about the summons and get angry all over again. After work, he picked up his daughter and drove around for a while, finally going to his apartment because he had to think. He sat and stared at his sleeping child. He loved her with all his heart. No one would ever separate them. He put his feelings in check, took a deep breath, and prepared to go home to Joy.

Joy had arrived home and found the place empty. She found it odd but brushed it off and started dinner. Brendan arrived shortly after she started cooking.

"Hi, there! What took you two so long?" Joy asked.

Before answering, he placed the baby in her portable crib and sat down on the sofa.

"I got a summons today."

"Really? For what?"

"Ms. Plummer is suing for custody of Brenda."

"What?" Joy screamed. "How could she? What right does she have? On what grounds?"

Brendan didn't respond. He simply handed her the documents to read for herself.

"She is requesting full custody and control of funds. What funds?" asked Joy.

"I don't know, but tomorrow I'm hiring a lawyer. This woman has lost her mind if she thinks she can take my child. I'll use every dime I have to fight this."

"Relax honey. I know that it will be okay."

"I can't relax."

"You have to. Don't let this upset you. This is our child, and she's not going anywhere!" Joy exclaimed.

Brendan looked up and watched her walk over to the phone. She picked up the handset and dialed. He sat up and listened to her side of the conversation.

"Mona? This is Joy Spicer. I need a lawyer. Child custody. Brenda McNair. That will be fine. Tuesday at noon? Fine, see you there." She disconnected the call and walked into the kitchen.

Brendan sat for a few minutes reveling in the feelings of love. He didn't miss her saying *our* child. She took it upon herself to secure a lawyer and proceeded to finish dinner; he definitely had a keeper. He relaxed and let his soon to be wife finish dinner.

***

Portia pulled off the wedding without Joy's help, and now she was Mrs. Brighton. She held her hand out and admired the large sparkler dominating her left hand. She leaned back in her oversized chair and admired her professionally decorated room. The first week of the marriage was wonderful. Her new husband was more than attentive. She felt like the luckiest woman in the world.

Hawaii was better than she could have imagined. During the day, she walked the beaches and shopped. Her nights were spent making love with her new husband. She had no reason to believe the honeymoon would ever end. Now that they had returned home a few days ago, she was settling into her new role.

She had her own suite filled with clothes and shoes. She wanted to add a few pieces of furniture, so she booted up her laptop. She was so engrossed in the online catalog that she didn't hear her husband come in.

"What are you doing?" he asked.

"Just ordering a few things," she said.

At that moment, a pop up caught his attention.

"So, you are talking to someone else? We've only been married a few days, and you're already cheating on me?" he asked.

Not realizing the seriousness of his tone, she replied, "Of course not. It's just a friend sending me a message."

"What kind of friend? You don't need friends. Everything you need is in this house!" he said.

Portia ignored his remarks. She turned her back to him and faced the screen to respond to her friend. She never saw the blow coming. He struck her so hard that she became dizzy. That was the first time he hit her, but it wasn't the last.

"Don't turn your back to me. I am talking to you," his voice came out in an evil roar.

She looked at her husband. When did he change into this monster? Her ears were ringing from the blow as she looked up at him. He turned and left the room.

Later in the week, Portia looked around at the same room and tried to find comfort in the plush and lavish furnishings. She now understood what her friend meant. She really did not know the man she married. She was so excited about the wedding she didn't stop to take time and think about the actual marriage and what it would be like. She never spent more than a night with him. Now, she'd pledged a lifetime.

Was it really worth it? Growing up poor, she always fantasized about being rich, having an endless supply of money, and not having to worry about bills, but now that she had time to think and reflect, she was always dressed in clean clothes, always had food to eat, and her family was actually happy. This was not happiness. She felt like a prisoner in her own house. It only took a few days for her to realize what a horrible mistake she made. Her happily ever after lasted about eight days. She walked over to the other side of the room and sat down on her vanity and expertly applied her makeup.

She wanted to make sure the bruises would not show through. She was careful with choosing her outfit to make sure nothing would reveal any of the bruises on her body. She took a long hard look at herself in the mirror and struggled with her emotions. She didn't have anyone to run to. It only took a few weeks for him to alienate the remainder of her few friends. Portia realized she was all alone.

"Are you ready to go?" her husband's voice startled her, causing her to drop the makeup brush she was holding.

"In just a moment, I'll be ready to go."

He walked over to her and took her hand and placed a kiss on her wrist. "You look beautiful, darling. I don't want us to be too late." He walked out of the room, and she watched him leave.

She finished her makeup and slid on her six thousand dollar dress. Tonight, she was expected to smile and nod. She wasn't to speak more words than it took to respond to any questions directed to her. She picked up her equally expensive purse and hurried downstairs to meet him. She never knew what to expect from him. Even though he was cordial, he could change instantly. Portia knew another thing. She had to find a way out.

Chapter 8

Tiffany finally got home and undressed. She really needed a car. Waiting thirty minutes on a ride was ridiculous. She rushed through a shower before going next door to pick up the kids. *Another day another dollar,* she thought to herself. Getting used to working took a few days, but she had to admit it felt good to be able to take care of herself. After her shower, she threw on a long, cotton dress and a pair of flip flops and headed next door.

"Ms. Murphy, it's Tiffany," she said as she knocked on the door. She was being careful not to trip over the many flower pots her neighbor had crowding the extremely small porch.

The elderly woman came to the door slowly.

"Hey baby, what's the matter?

"I'm here to get my kids," Tiffany said with a confused look on her face.

"They daddy came 'bout an hour ago, baby," the elderly woman replied in a shaky voice.

"What? Why did you let him take them?" she asked instantly panicking.

"I didn't know he couldn't take 'em," the elderly woman replied.

"Okay, okay," Tiffany said and backed away.

Ms. Murphy closed the door.

Panicking, Tiffany turned and tripped on the hem of her dress. She fell hard hitting the concrete. Slowly, she stood and steadied herself. She slowly went back to her apartment. Reggie knew she did not have a car. Even if she did, she had no idea where he was.

Feeling even more foolish, she realized she had two children with him and didn't know where he lived. When she was married to Slim, she would meet Reggie at a motel. Once she got her divorce, he would just stay a few days with her. Tiffany felt helpless; she had no idea where he was or when he would return her children. Why would he even do this?

Realizing she was bleeding, she went to the bathroom to clean her wounds. She called her mother and told her what happened, and her mother promised to come as soon as she could.

Tiffany had no idea where Reggie was staying. Even if she did, she had no way of getting there. When they divorced, Slim took back her car. She wanted to call the police but wasn't sure if it would do any good. They were his kids, after all. She began to panic.

Tiffany started pacing the floor when there was a knock at the door. A woman she never saw before was standing there with her babies. She had her son by the hand, and the baby was in her carrier. Tiffany scooped them up while demanding to know who she was and how she got her children.

The woman calmly stated that Reggie had brought them to her house and that he had left. "You may want to get a restraining order. File a report or something. Get the law involved. He is more dangerous than you know. I knew that these were your kids, and I know he was here a lot. I had him tailed a while back." The woman noticed Tiffany had a confused look on her face. "So, you didn't know?"

"Know what?" she snapped.

"Reggie is married."

"Married?"

"Yea, married," the woman said throwing up her left hand to illustrate. "You aren't the only one. He has three outside children that I know of," she said sadly.

They stared at each other for a few tense seconds, then the woman turned and walked away. Tiffany stood in her doorway. She was completely dumbfounded. It was at that moment she knew she had to get away from Reggie.

***

After work, Brendan decided to run by his apartment and get a few things and check the mail. He was locking up when Tiffany pulled up in her mom's car.

"What can I do for you?" he asked.

"Slim, can I come in, please?"

"What do you want? I'm leaving."

"Reggie took my kids while I was at work and…"

"Tiffany, get to the point."

"You don't even care, do you?" she asked.

"You took my kids. Do you remember that? You had me believing I had a son and a daughter on the way, and you took them, leaving me feeling like I'd never have a relationship with them. Look, I don't know why you came here, but I am done with you. Completely done. You made a fool of me once, never again. Go and find a new sucker." Brendan walked away leaving her standing there.

Tiffany walked back to the car and watched him drive away. *Damn,* she thought. *I messed up a good thing running behind Reggie.* Slim was right; she only had herself to blame. She sat in the car and thought. She had hoped he would let her use his car for a while until she got on her feet. He had always helped her when she needed it. She had to depend on herself from now on. She drove to the police station and placed a complaint and then hurried home to her children. Her mother had fed and bathed them, and they were playing happily. Tiffany thanked her mom and sat down with a plop.

"Tiffany, what are you going to do now?

"Not sure, Momma. These are his children, but he had no right to take them without my knowledge. I have no idea what he may do."

"So, you haven't seen him?" her mother asked, getting up to get the baby.

"No, not since the other day when he tried to get a key," Tiffany responded.

"How did you get bruised up?"

"Oh, I fell. I was so shaken up that I tripped on Ms. Murphy's front step," she said as she flopped down on the sofa.

"Are you sure? It looks like you lost a fight," replied her mother.

"Yes, Mom, I fell."

"Well, just thank God that it's Friday. Maybe it will look better on Monday."

Tiffany took a look at herself, and the bruises had started turning dark purple and were more pronounced. She definitely looked like she had been in a fight. Tiffany used the weekend to search for a car. Taking her mother's advice, she reached out to her father. He agreed to let her have one of his. It wasn't new, but it was dependable. Having transportation made her feel more independent, and it was a feeling she liked. However, with a car came extra financial responsibility. She would need insurance, maintenance, and gas money. Baring these things in mind, she needed to find a way to earn more money.

***

Monday morning Joy reluctantly got up for work. Thankfully, the baby had slept through most of the night. She dressed and got the baby ready. After dropping her off at daycare, she picked up a breakfast combo from a nearby chain restaurant. She needed an assistant but hadn't had time to train one. She thought about promoting from within, but the clerks she had were mostly college students, two of whom were graduating soon and would need replacing.

Joy was facing another busy day. Her mother's impromptu visit ruined her plans to do any work Sunday. She was just going to have to delegate some of the work for a while. She had started working when a knock on the door broke her concentration.

"Come in."

"Good morning."

"Well, good morning, Tiffany. What can I do for you?"

Tiffany removed her baseball cap and looked her in the eye.

"What happened to you?" Joy asked with concern.

"I fell—really I did. I wanted to talk to you about getting more hours. I know that my hours are based on the occupancy, but I need to be able to care for my children and me. My ex took my kids, and I couldn't do anything. I had to wait until my mom came to let me use her car. I just want to be able to care for us. I don't want to feel helpless."

"I understand. Did you talk to your supervisor?"

"Yes, I did, but she already hired new people, so she doesn't have any extra hours available."

Joy leaned back and thought for a moment.

"I think I have something in mind for you, but as of now the laundry is behind so you can clock in now if you want, and I will get back with you around one o'clock, okay?"

"That will be great, thanks." Tiffany clocked in and headed to the laundry room. The desk clerk stared at the bruises and scratches but didn't say anything. Tiffany didn't volunteer any information, and no one was brave enough to ask. It was nobody's business anyway.

She was glad she came in early to talk to Joy. She needed the extra hours. She hoped she would give her more hours permanently. She knew that from now on she would have to take care of herself. She had only been working a few minutes when she got a call to come up front. The clerk assured her that it wasn't Reggie.

Joy was deep into her work when she got a call from the front desk letting her know the police were there looking for Tiffany. Joy stepped out of her office to witness the encounter.

"Tiffany McNair?" asked the larger of the two officers.

"Yes," she answered, instantly nervous seeing two uniformed policemen.

"We need to ask you a few questions."

"Okay, what about? Oh about the restraining order?" she asked.

"No, ma'am. This is about an attempted murder."

"How did you get that bruise?" asked the other officer.

"I fell," she stated.

"Miss, lying to the police is a..." started the other officer.

"I fell. Why is it so hard to believe that I fell? I tripped on the tail of my dress and fell on the concrete steps. Okay, so tell me what's going on."

"Reginald Hall," stated the cop taking the notes.

"He tried to kill someone?" Tiffany asked.

"Ma'am, he was shot Friday by a female. Where were you between the hours of three and six?" the officer asked.

"You think I shot him? I haven't seen that bastard. I was at the police station filing an incident report because he took my children. I didn't get off until 4:30 on Friday. When the sitter told me he had taken them, I panicked and turned too fast that's why I fell."

"What is your relation to him?" the officer asked.

"I have two children with him, but we are no longer together. Why are you asking me anyway? Why aren't you asking his wife or his other baby momma?"

The two officers exchanged looks and seemed satisfied with her answers. They left but warned her she was not off the hook yet. Tiffany was sure she would be completely cleared because she was innocent. However, she wondered what woman shot Reggie.

***

Laying in pain Reggie tried to get comfortable on the narrow hospital bed. His vision was blurry. He kept trying to focus but found it to be impossible. He could hear the beep of the monitors. He tried hard to focus on the objects in the room, but he couldn't make out much. He gave up and tried to sleep. When he woke again, the nurse was in the room.

"I can't see straight," he complained to the nurse.

"It's the medicine. It will clear up soon."

He closed his eyes and slept. When Reggie woke again, he had no idea what time it was or how long he had been in the hospital. His body ached, and his mouth felt like it was full of cotton. He needed water so he pressed the nurse button and waited.

"Yes, sir."

"Water, please."

The same nurse came in and helped him down a cold cup of water. He thanked her and tried to get comfortable. There was pain, but it was bearable. He knew that he was in the hospital. He was trying to remember how he got there. He slowly remembered what happened, and he still couldn't believe she shot him.

Chapter 9

Carolyn took on the task of clearing out her sister's house. Her mother was insisting on an estate sale. She would have had one, but she found out she didn't have the right to do so. The house, money and other vehicle belonged to Brenda. Her sister's life insurance policy originally had their mother as the beneficiary; however, it was changed once she got pregnant. After the funeral, they found out her will was revised as well. Vanessa was always a planner. Her untimely death left her daughter quite wealthy.

Carolyn took her time and went through each room and boxed her personal papers and belongings. She saved the nursery for last. She boxed all the clothes and shower gifts, most of which hadn't been opened or used. Once she finished, she fished out Brendan's number and dialed.

"Hello."

"Hi Brendan, this is Carolyn. I just boxed up all the babies things. I thought that you would want them."

"Well, yes of course. But why are you offering?"

"What do you mean? They do belong to her."

"Did you know that your mother is trying to take custody of the baby?" Brendan asked.

"No, I didn't know. I mean, she never said anything to me about it. I know she is still distraught. It is tough losing a child," Carolyn told him.

"I don't know if it's grief or greed," he replied.

"What do you mean by that?"

"She is requesting control of the money and property that Vanessa left to Brenda."

"I'm sorry. I don't know what to say, but I'll send the baby's things."

"Thanks, Carolyn, I really appreciate that."

After making the arrangements for the boxes, she hung up. Carolyn went back to Vanessa's bedroom. She had grouped all of her papers and notebooks together without looking at any. She decided she would do some digging. After she found what she needed, she decided to include those boxes with the shipment of the baby's things.

Mrs. Plumber felt justified in her actions truly believing that Brendan was the cause of her daughter's demise. She thought he should suffer. As far as she was concerned, he didn't deserve the right to raise the baby, let alone reap the benefits from Vanessa's death. She was her mother and the money, houses, and car should be hers. The whistle blew on her teapot breaking her train of thought.

She poured the boiling hot liquid in her cup and took a seat in a nearby chair. She sweetened her drink and added a little milk to cool it down a bit. She extended her foot and looked at her worn, brown house slippers and smirked thinking she would soon be able to replace them. She thought of all the things she would buy and do with the money. She fantasized for a few minutes thinking she could regularly take cruises without having to save for months.

She stood, stretched, and grabbed her mug. She had decided to go and do a little shopping, so she went to get dressed. As she walked towards her bedroom, she hummed a little tune. Mrs. Plumber gleefully turned the corner and fell flat on her face sending her cup flying one way and her raggedy slippers another.

Luckily, Carolyn decided to confront her mother after finding the insurance papers. She had an idea as to why she now wanted custody. It was only a few minutes' drive, but she couldn't get there fast enough. She couldn't believe her mother would do such a thing. *Money sure changes things.*

Carolyn knocked first then let herself in. The house was eerily quiet. Instantly alarmed, she called out to her mother. She did not get a response which worried her more. She looked in the kitchen then headed towards her mother's room. She found her mother sprawled out on the bedroom floor.

"Mom, can you hear me?"

"Yeah, I just fell. This damn slipper caught on something, and it must have knocked me out for a minute or two."

"Okay, okay, you scared me half to death. Can you walk?"

"Not sure. Can you help me up?" her mother asked. With Carolyn's assistance, she was able to stand but only for a few seconds. "My foot! Oh my goodness!" she said with her voice shaking in anguish.

Carolyn looked down and saw the purplish bruise covering her mother's foot.

"Mom, I think you have sprained your ankle," she said then added, "Well, I guess God don't like ugly."

"What do you mean by that?"

Carolyn was busy gathering her mother's purse and keys. She ignored her mother's question and said, "Come on, Mom. You need to get to the emergency room."

The doctor confirmed her ankle was sprained. He wrapped her foot and prescribed pain medicine. Grateful it was only a sprain, Carolyn helped her mother into the car and drove to the nearby pharmacy to pick up her pain medicine. Ms. Plummer sat silently in the passenger seat. Once Carolyn got her home, she gave her the medicine and waited for her to go to sleep.

Once her mom was asleep, she did a little snooping. She found remodeling estimates and travel brochures. Obviously, her mother was making plans. Her sister wasn't even cold yet, and all her mother wanted to do was spend Vanessa's money. Vanessa wasn't rich, but she planned well. Her teacher's salary did not afford her all that she had. Smart and frugal, she purchased a few foreclosed properties and rented them out. The monthly payments she received in rent allowed her to have the house she wanted.

Carolyn put the papers back and shoved the drawer closed. She heard something fall. She opened the cabinet and saw the letter that fell. She started to put it back but noticed how old it looked. It must have been stuck behind the drawer for a while. She laid it in the drawer and realized it was addressed to her. The envelope beckoned her to open it, but for some reason, she was apprehensive.

She looked at the date stamped over the envelope almost twenty-three years ago. The letter had gotten stuck behind the drawer soon after they moved into the house. She opened the envelope, and a small rectangle slip of paper fell to the floor. She bent down and retrieved the sheet of paper. It was a receipt. Suddenly, that day's events began to replay in her mind.

Carolyn began to remember the physical pain, mental anguish, and embarrassment as she had stood next to her mother who was bouncing with excitement. Carolyn, who had gritty eyes and felt sore from the recent procedure, stood quietly beside her mother. Her mother who had been short-tempered and downright mean the last few months was unusually happy that day.

The plump receptionist asked, "Miss Palmer, my system is down. Do you mind if I mail you a receipt?"

"That's fine, and it's Plummer. P-l-u-m-m-e-r," she replied, spelling out her last name.

Carolyn remembered that they had just moved back to town into the new house. Where did all the money come from? They had been struggling, especially with Vanessa in college. She decided it was time to do some digging. She took advantage of the fact that her mother was in a deep pain med induced sleep. She pulled opened cabinets and drawers. She went through files, and she searched in boxes. She did not leave any stones unturned. After a few hours, she gave up and put everything back the way she found it. While putting back a box in the closet shelf, a single sheet fell to the floor. She realized it was an old bank statement. *Momma never throws away anything*, she thought to herself.

She looked for a few minutes but could not tell where the piece of paper came from. Finally, she went to retrieve a footstool to get a better view. She saw there was a flat folder on the shelf. In the folder, she found house papers and a bank statement from that month. There was the canceled check from the down payment. She took the folder and put the footstool back in the place. Finally, Carolyn had her answers.

Chapter 10

Now that her weekend would be free, Joy reached out to a friend and booked a weekend getaway. She felt they needed a few days away. The baby, Vanessa's funeral, and now the pending court case were weighing heavily on them both. She was getting dressed while Brendan was out picking up a few items for the baby and gassing up the car.

A few miles away, Tristan finished with his last appointment then showered and shaved. He grabbed a clean shirt on his way out the door. He pulled up to the barbershop and waited on his turn. He had decided to talk to Joy. He couldn't let it go any longer. She hadn't called him in over a month. He hoped he hadn't waited too late.

After a new cut, Tristan felt like a new man. He went home to change then drove the few miles to her house. He was in her driveway when he thought, *Dang I should have gotten her flowers or something, but I'm here now.* He knocked on the door.

The sight of her made him do a double take. Her hair was combed away from her face and flowing down her back and shoulders. She was wearing a thin strapped black dress that showed off her curves.

"What's up?" she asked with a smile that made him want to grab her and kiss her right there on the doorstep. She opened the door wider and invited him in. He followed her into the living room.

"Looks like you're going out. Are you and Portia going somewhere?" he asked hopefully. "Or, is it the new guy?" he asked, trying to keep his voice normal.

"Portia and I are no longer friends, and I don't want to talk about it. So, what brings you by today?"

"I wanted to talk to you, but I think this is a bad time."

"I have a few minutes before Brendan gets back home. What's up, Tristan? You never just drop by."

"I'll come back."

"No, come on sit by me and spill it!"

He looked at her and blurted, "I love you."

"I love you too," she said looking confused.

"No, I *love* you," he said while getting closer and grabbing her hands. "I am in love with you. I should have told you a long time ago. Long before you married Morris. I messed up and never should have let you go back in college. I never got over you. I never got over us and what we shared. I needed you to know."

Joy was too stunned to speak. She was frozen in place staring at him when Tristan leaned in and kissed her.

"What the hell is going on here?" Brendan asked, his voice bouncing off the walls.

Joy stood motionlessly as Brendan walked farther into the room. When she found her voice, she heard herself say, "Nothing." Having no idea that Tristan still had feelings for her, she was stunned. She stood and distanced herself from him.

"Don't look like nothing to me," said Brendan in a low, menacing tone.

Tristan looked up to her and gave her a pleading look, which she ignored. Feeling lost, he dropped his head. "Nothing man, just like she said. I was mistaken."

At that moment, Brenda made her presence known. Joy started towards her room, but Slim stopped her.

"No, let her cry a minute, so you can tell me why that man was kissing you. Why did I come home to this?"

"This is not what it looks like," Joy explained.

"I'm going to check on the baby. He needs to be gone when I get back," Brendan said and walked away.

"You need to leave now, Tristan," Joy said to her long-time friend.

"I didn't mean to cause a problem. I just wanted you to know how I felt."

"Tristan, please." She walked over to the door and opened it.

Tristan quietly left. He got into his car and drove off. He was pulling into his driveway when he realized her boyfriend had said 'home.' Was the dude living with her?

What happened to Portia? Why were they no longer friends? Where did that baby come from? His head began to ache from all the unanswered questions.

***

Claire pulled up to Joy's house a few minutes after the incident. *Not bad,* she thought to herself taking in the exterior. She knocked and admired the beautiful landscaping while she waited to be let in. Brendan soon opened the door. Even though he tried to hide it, she knew that something was wrong. Not wanting to be nosey, she ignored it. They gave her the numbers and a spare key and left. Whatever it was, she hoped they worked it out before returning. She felt Joy was right for him.

The tension between them was thick enough to cut with a knife. There were three hours between them and their destination. Joy wasn't sure what to say so she said nothing. They rode in silence for twenty minutes. His anger had dissipated some, so he broke the silence with, "Who is he?"

She let out a breath and replied, "He is just a friend."

"Who is he really, Joy?

"I grew up with him."

"So, you have never been intimate with him?"

"We dated briefly in college."

"So, let me get this straight. A man you have been intimate with was in the house while I was gone?"

"Nothing happened. He only kissed me."

"Only?"

"Brendan, I am sorry, but nothing happened. I had no idea he still had feelings for me. We have been friends for years. We practically grew up together. I did nothing wrong."

Brendan continued driving. He knew he wasn't dealing with Tiffany, but still, he didn't want to subject himself to any more disappointment. Joy reached out and placed her hand on his. He turned his hand over and intertwined their fingers.

"I'm sorry that I blew up Joy, but I won't go through that again."

"I know how you feel. Brendan, I would not intentionally hurt you in any way. You should know that by now."

"I believe you. You are right. I should have known better. Let's just drop it. We are taking this trip to get away from drama for a few days."

They spent the rest of the drive making future plans. Once they arrived at the hotel, the incident was all but forgotten. The hotel was more than he imagined. It was hidden away from the main road. If the interior was anything like the exterior, he knew they were in for a treat. Brendan had to be careful not to look like a kid on his first Disney trip.

"Thanks for this, Joy," he said in awe as they headed to the front door.

"We really needed it," she said with a shrug.

"Yes, we did," he replied, running his hands over her behind.

"The past few months have been rough," she admitted.

"I know, and I will make it up to you—thoroughly."

Clearly getting his meaning, she gave him a seductive smile and said, "You better."

As agreed, there was no more talk about court, work or exes. The first night they took advantage of the hot tub. Brendan felt a bit out of place, but Joy seemed to be right at home.

"How did you know about this place?"

"I know the owner," she said between sips of champagne.

"Oh, so you are just well connected, huh?"

"Something like that," she said with a soft laugh. "Come on, let's get dressed and go to dinner."

"As long as you let me have you for dessert," he teased.

"That is a deal."

They entered the dining room and found a table along the wall. The tables surrounded a large dance floor. During dinner, they watched couples dance while they enjoyed the expertly prepared meal.

"Can you dance?" she asked

"No, not this kind of dancing."

"I can teach you."

"Maybe later."

Heading to their suite after dinner, an older gentleman approached them.

"Young man, you look just like my younger brother when he was younger. The resemblance is amazing."

"Well, they say we all have a twin," Brendan replied and started to walk away.

"If you don't mind, let me show you something." The gentleman pulled out his wallet and handed him a folded picture of a man that looked just like him.

A chill ran through Slim's body.

"Oh, my goodness, Brendan. He looks just like you," Joy said in astonishment.

"I agree. Too much like me," Brendan said. "Does your brother have any children?" he asked the man.

"No, his wife wasn't able to have any. Why do you ask?"

"No reason. Well, I mean, I never met my father. I don't even know his name or whether he is dead or alive." Brendan looked at the picture again and unfolded it to reveal two more young men. "Who are they?"

"That's me in the middle and my other brother," the man said.

Joy leaned in and gasped. "That's Mr. Harold; Tristan's dad."

"You know my nephew?"

"Yes, sir, I grew up with him."

Recognition made him step back. "You are Roger's little girl."

"Yes, sir."

"You don't remember me I know, but your dad and I were good friends," he said to Joy then turned back to Brendan. "Son, it was nice to meet you. By the way, what is your mother's name?"

"Claire McNair."

The man's expression became serious as he extended his hand. "My name is James Cunningham. I believe that I am your uncle." He pulled Brendan in and hugged him tight then released him. Taking the picture, he gave him a card. He had Brendan to write his info on the back of another. "I'll be in touch," he said starting to walk away.

Brendan nodded then shouted "Wait! What's his name?"

"Walt Cunningham."

Later in the room, Joy tried to console him. She could tell he was having a hard time processing the information. Brendan didn't know how to feel. His mother never said a word. A complete stranger he met by chance gave him more information than she had.

"I'm okay, baby," he said with a tight smile.

She placed her head on his shoulder. "Are you sure?"

"Yes, I am," he said and placed a kiss on her forehead.

She helped him out of his shirt and positioned herself behind him and slowly massaged his shoulders until she felt him began to relax. "Okay, now lay back and get some rest," she urged him.

He did and quickly fell asleep.

Joy couldn't sleep, and even after a hot shower, she was still very much awake. If Walt really was his father, then he and Tristan were first cousins. The man she affectionately referred to as Uncle Walt could possibly be Slim's father. Why didn't she notice the resemblance? She felt like she needed to tell him all that she knew, but what if he wasn't his father? Should she wait? But if she waited and he found out how well she knew him, then what? Tired of thinking, she finally fell asleep.

Joy had scheduled massages for them and a pedicure for herself. In addition to the spa, the hotel had a small casino, pool, and tennis court. The city had great shopping, theaters, dining, and clubs minutes away. She had planned to cram it all in those two days, but after last night's encounter, she didn't think Brendan would be up to it.

He surprised her by waking up full of energy. After breakfast and the spa, they went out to explore the city. Joy suggested they stop at a bar and grill in the city for lunch. Over lunch, he brought up the dreaded subject.

"So, do you know Walt?"

"Yes, I met him at Tristan's house. He came by often."

Several tense seconds went by before he asked, "Do you have any idea where he lives?"

"Yes, I have been there a few times. But that was back in college."

Slim laid down his menu and looked at her.

"Unless they moved, the house is close by if you want to go."

"Yeah, I think I do."

"Okay, we can go after lunch."

"No, I don't want to go today," he said, suddenly changing his mind. "I want to spend this weekend with you. I don't know the circumstances that led my mother to keep me away from him. After I talk to her, I'll decide. Now pretty lady, let's eat so I can take you out on the town."

"Sounds like a plan."

***

Finally back in the room, they were able to relax. The day had taken its toll on both of them. Instead of having dinner out, they ordered room service. After appeasing their hunger, the exhausted couple fell asleep watching a movie on TV. Joy was the first to wake. She decided to take a shower and wash away the long day. She was busy getting herself lathered up when she felt a cold draft. She turned slowly to watch him step into the shower. She smiled at the sight of his hard body. Words were not necessary.

He took the sponge and finished the job for her. She let him soap her body. The gentle swipes of the sponge began to arouse her. She turned and let him lather her back and shoulders. Slowly, he made his way down her body. He turned her around so that she was facing him and began kissing her deeply. Caught up in the heat of the moment, he let the sponge fall. Swiftly, he lifted her as if she was weightless. Slowly, he eased his manhood inside her. Brendan kept his promise and thoroughly made love to her. The water on her back and the man sliding in and out of her sent her over the edge within minutes. Her hoarse cry was barely heard over the flowing water and rhythmic slaps of their thighs. Finally, thoroughly pleased, they retired to the bed.

With the weekend over, it was time to face the real world. After a pancake breakfast Sunday morning, they checked out of the hotel and headed home. Both were relatively quiet, each lost in thought. Brendan was inwardly dealing with a newfound knowledge of Walt Cunningham. Knowing his mother as well as he did, he knew she had a reason for keeping him ignorant of his father's name and whereabouts. He desperately wanted to question her, but he was hesitant to do so. He had made up his mind to wait.

Joy was reassessing her life. After the weekend, she realized the freedom she had grown accustomed to while single was now nonexistent. Having a man was one thing, but a baby was another. No more simple things such as sleeping late. Brenda awoke every morning by six demanding to be fed and/or changed. After work, she had to go straight home and cook or finish another household chore. Taking a bubble bath or any self-serving activity had to wait until the baby was asleep.

As much as she loved them, she did have to wonder if she was doing the right thing. She had to wonder if she was taking on too much responsibility too fast. Even though she was far from being broke, spending thousands of dollars for weekend getaways could not happen every week. She realized she needed a break, and she really needed to talk to Brendan about that, but she didn't want him to feel like she was unhappy. She was simply tired.

"Joy, what's wrong? Joy, why do you have that strange look on your face?" he asked.

"I'm just thinking."

"About what?" After a few moments of silence, he asked again. "Joy, what are you thinking about? Please talk to me."

"I think I need a break, Brendan."

"What's wrong? We just had a..."

"Overnight," she said, cutting him off. "I have a man and a child. I have more responsibilities at work since I have gone from being the assistant to being completely in charge. When I come home, I'm still on the go. There isn't any relief. We can't do weekend getaways every week. I would like to at least sleep late on the weekends or on my days off. I can't do that now. I just need a small break, that's all. I'm just tired. I have taken on a lot all of a sudden without time to get myself prepared for it."

Brendan patiently listened.

"You're right. Look, I'll just move out for a while and give you some space."

"Brendan. I didn't mean…" she started.

"No," he cut her off. "You're right. I didn't even ask. I just moved in with a newborn. She is my responsibility. It was too much too soon."

"Brendan, look," she said trying again to interrupt.

"No, Joy, you've been more than supportive. I never thought about it from your point of view. Let's slow it down a bit and give us both some time to adjust. This is not a breakup, just a step back for a while, okay?"

"Brendan, where are you going to go?"

"I can go to my apartment. I have at least two more months on the lease so I can stay there. All my furniture is there. I'll be fine."

"Okay, what about our wedding? Are we still getting married?"

"Nothing else has changed, Joy. Actually, this may give us time to miss each other."

She let out a sigh and finally conceded.

"Thanks for understanding, Brendan."

"No, thank you for putting up with my baby and me for this long." He reached out and grabbed her hand. "Joy, I love you more than I ever thought possible. You were there for me when I needed it most. When you are ready, and only then we can move back in, okay?"

"Okay." She gave his hand a squeeze and reclined her seat.

Chapter 11

James Cunningham pulled up to his brother's house early Sunday morning. His sister-n-law came to the door after a few knocks.

"Good morning, James. Come on in. He is in the kitchen," she said.

"Thanks, Belle."

His brother, Walt, was sitting at the table working on a stack of pancakes. "What brings you by this early, old man?" asked Walt.

"Claire McNair," he said and placed the card on the table.

"Claire died a long time ago. Why are you bringing her up now?" Walt asked.

James shook his head from side to side. Walt looked up at him in confusion. He looked down at the card and then back up to his brother.

"Your son," James said then looked his brother in the eye and turned and walked out the way he came.

Walt stood, emptied his plate in the trash can, and cleared the table. He pushed up his chair and swept around the table. He was busy loading the dishwasher when he noticed the housekeeper staring at him.

"Are you okay, Mr. Cunningham?" she asked with a look of concern on her face.

"Yes, I'm fine, Pearl," he replied. He was so deep in thought he didn't realize he was cleaning.

"Maybe you need to have a seat, sir," she said, taking the plate away from him.

"I'm fine, Pearl, just got something on my mind." He sank into a nearby chair. The conversation with his brother was still on his mind. He had a son. Claire was alive, and so was their child. He was having a hard time processing the information. He didn't know whether to laugh or cry.

All this time, he believed she was dead. Claire's sweet face came to mind along with the pain of losing her all of those years ago. She was alive, and so was the child. He couldn't believe it. Why didn't she contact him? There were so many unanswered questions. He didn't want to be hasty, so he decided to do some detecting before using the information his brother gave him.

The memories of her came flooding back. He sat in his study and let her image come to mind. The sweet, innocent smile and the way she carried herself were the two things that caused him to fall in love with her. Even though he was already married, he was not in love with his wife. His father insisted that he marry Belle to further the family business. Being the obedient son that he was, he did what his father asked. Over the years, he developed a fondness for Belle, but Claire had his heart. It took several years to get over Claire.

Walt exhaled and leaned back in his easy chair. A son. He had a son. Claire had given him a son. He sat and let his mind go back to the last time they were together.

"Come on. Girl. Ride with me!" said a very young Walt.

"I can't go now. My ma— job needs me," she said catching herself before saying 'my mom.' She didn't want to sound too young. She was careful not to let it slip that she was only sixteen.

"Oh, come on. I have to go out of town for three weeks," he pleaded.

Claire got one of the girls to cover for her and jumped in the car.

Walt wanted to tell her how he felt but knew she wouldn't understand the situation. He was married. Not happily, but he was married all the same. He did not love his wife, but he loved the money and security that came with being married to her. His father made it clear that he wanted him to marry Belle. It made sense—dollars and cents. He was sure his wife was aware of his affairs, but this one was different. He loved Claire.

He took Claire shopping that day and later to his hotel. He remembered how happy she was trying on all the new things he'd purchased for her. He liked making her happy. The time passed too soon for them. It was time to take her back, and he had to go home to his wife.

He never saw Claire again. Once he returned from his business trip, he received a frantic phone call from her saying she was pregnant and needed to see him. She never showed up.

Walt was so deep in thought that he didn't hear his wife come into the room. She was standing in front of him. She had the card in her hand. There was a look of defeat on her face.

"What is it, Belle? What's wrong?"

She dropped her head. Her body language gave it all away. He remembered she was the one that told him Claire was dead. She was the one that read the newspaper clipping to him.

"The newspaper was a fake. Wasn't it?"

"Yes."

"How did you even know about her?"

"I heard you and your brother talking about it. Did you even know or even care that she was sixteen years old." Her expression answered the question for him. "You didn't know?"

"Belle, what did you do?"

"How dare you take that tone with me. You are *my* husband," she angrily replied.

"Belle, please."

"Well, husband, her name badge was in your luggage. I did some digging and found her. A waitress, Walt? Really? When I confronted her, I realized she had no idea I existed. But guess how surprised I was to find out that she was pregnant."

"Belle, you know our marriage was more or less arranged. You didn't love me. I mean, our parents…"

"I did love you. I have always loved you," she shouted cutting him off. "I wanted to give you children too, but a sixteen-year-old fast-food waitress..." she stopped mid-sentence and sat down as the tears ran down her face.

The couple sat and stared at each other for a few moments. Walt was beginning to see things through her eyes. He understood her pain. All the years he'd resented the marriage, he realized he never gave the marriage or her a chance. He had a woman that loved him, but being selfish, he never tried to love her back. It was a marriage of convenience, but it didn't have to be.

Walt looked at his wife. They had been married for more than forty years, and he finally realized his mistake. He stood and walked over to her. He gathered her into his arms.

"I'm sorry," he said. Believing she didn't love him, he never let himself love her. He had multiple affairs and told himself he did what his father asked and didn't need to do anymore. Belle could have left years ago. He realized she did love him, and he was just refusing to see it. "Can we start over?" he asked her.

She tearfully nodded her head yes. That night after forty years of marriage Walt Cunningham made love to his wife.

Tonya

Chapter 12

The boxes for Brenda had arrived a few days after the weekend getaway, and Joy was anxious to get her room finished. The contractor had completed the room a few days ago. She had a doorway cut between her office space and Brenda's room to create a playroom easily accessible from the nursery. The walk-in closet was also updated. Joy had shelves added for more storage. It had been a few weeks, and she did miss Brendan and the baby, but the break had to happen. She saw them regularly, but no overnight visits since the getaway. He was right; the time apart was just what they needed.

The next day, Joy finished up the deposit and entered her employees' hours to complete payroll. She had decided to leave early. She was missing her family and wanted to go by Brendan's apartment. She pressed the power button on her computer and reached for her purse. She looked up as Tristan casually walked into her office.

Tristan walked into her office determined to plead his case. Feeling he was the better choice, he was determined to make her see the light.

"Joy, can you please hear me out?"

"Tristan, don't," she stated, putting her hand up.

"I just want to talk to you. May I have a few minutes?"

"Go ahead."

"Look, what does he have to offer you?"

"Tristan, if you think you can downgrade him to make yourself seem more appealing, then you are mistaken."

"I'm sorry; that was not my intention. I should not have said that. I'm sorry I caused you any distress. I love you very much, and I should have said something a long time ago."

"Tristan, I do love you but only as a friend, nothing more. The very brief time we were together is gone. I am happy, Tristan. He makes me happy."

"How? I mean what does he do to make you happy? He is living off of you. I know this because I spoke to Portia if you remember her. She is a lifelong friend that you ditched because of him. He is clearly taking advantage of your good nature. I mean you…"

"GET OUT!" she yelled, shocking them both.

He stood frozen at the door.

"You heard me," she said.

"So, you are going to end our friendship, too? Just throw me aside like you did Portia?"

"I'm not having this conversation today. Leave."

"What about all that we had? What about our baby? What about the life we planned. I know I messed up, but I was immature and unable to handle the responsibilities that came with that situation."

"That gullible little girl that you knew died when you let our child die."

"We agreed not to place blame, and besides, we found our way back to each other, Joy."

"We were able to retain our friendship. As of now, I don't think we even have that." She pulled her purse strap up onto her shoulder and added, "After you."

Accepting defeat, Tristan walked out of the room.

Joy locked the door and headed home. She hadn't thought about or spoken to Portia since their last fight and wondered how she was doing now that she was married. She did miss her friend and felt maybe she had overreacted. She wished she had someone to talk to.

***

Brendan found out just how demanding Brenda could be after two days. He was exhausted. Two weeks was long enough to teach him a good lesson, such as with a newborn there was no such thing as a quick run to the store. He didn't think he would make it another week alone. That was totally out of the question. He needed help. He thought that maybe his mother would be able to help him out. He picked up his daughter and held her close, and as he inhaled her unique baby scent, he began to relax a little.

He picked up the phone and called Joy's cell phone.

"Hey, baby," she answered.

"Hey, what time are you leaving today?" he asked.

"I'm already home."

"Oh," he said.

"Brendan."

"Yes, baby."

"Come on home."

"We'll be there in a few."

Brendan packed up the car and prepared to head to Joy's house. He went back inside to pick up the baby when there was a knock.

"Hey, man," said his cousin as he walked in.

"Junior! It's been a minute."

"Man, it's been more than that. Where have you been? I stopped by several times, but you weren't here."

"I've been staying over my lady's house."

"Man, you've been missing about three to four months. She got you sprung like that?"

"Man, I'm marrying her as soon as possible."

"Damn, I didn't know it was like that. So, what happened to that other girl back home? The pregnant one. Was the baby yours?" Junior asked.

Slim smiled and walked over and picked up the car seat.

"Yeah. Meet Brenda McNair."

Junior dropped into a nearby chair.

"Well now. How are you dealing with that? I mean, she lived back in my old hometown. So, she let you keep the baby for a while? Or did she move up here? Wait!

How is your new lady taking all this? Has Vanessa been giving you any static?"

"Vanessa's dead, Junior."

"What? What happened? Did she die having the baby?"

"No, she was in a car wreck shortly after having the baby. It was in the local paper. You probably heard about the lady that got hit by an eighteen-wheeler."

"It was her? Man, I never would have thought that was her. I heard about that accident. How are you holding up, cuz?"

"I'm good. Joy has been great. I'm headed there now. The baby has a nursery over there, and we're pretty much living together until we get married. I was just here giving her a break 'cause newborn babies ain't no joke."

"Wow, man, I didn't know you were going through all of this."

"Look, let me give you her address, so you can stop by and holler at me sometimes. I'm going to go ahead and let this apartment go."

"I understand, man, it's like that when you find the right one."

"This time, I did man. I found a lady."

***

Tiffany left the police station with a huge grin on her face. She was no longer under suspicion. Relief flooded her body. As it turned out, Reggie's wife had pulled the trigger. According to the statement given by his friend, Reggie's wife came home to him changing the baby's diaper. When she asked him whose baby it was, he had responded 'mine.'

She calmly walked out of the room and retrieved her handgun. He laughed in her face, and she opened fire. His buddy forced him out of the house. His friend was a block away before he realized Reggie had been shot.

Tiffany was relieved but also concerned. She thought about the fact that her kids were there during that ordeal. She didn't want Reggie to die, but she needed to distance herself from him. She thanked God his wife brought the kids home. She knew she had to pay for the mistakes she had made; however, she did not want her children to hurt in the process. She still had no idea why Reggie took the children in the first place. What was his motive? What was his plan?

Maybe it was just a scare tactic or a way to force her to let him back into the house again; she didn't know. She felt like maybe she needed to move, especially since his wife knew where she lived. She had no idea the woman delivering her children to her had just shot someone.

She drove to her mom's house to pick up her children. She no longer left the children with her neighbor. Reggie was recovering and would be released soon. She felt the children were better off with her mother.

"Hi, Mom, how were they?"

"Fine," she replied as she packed the baby's bag.

"I went by the police station because they had called me. They could have just left a message, but anyway, it was his wife that shot him."

"What?"

"Yes, the lady that brought my kids to me had just shot him. Momma, I got to get away from that crazy man."

"What are you planning to do?"

"Move for one. I mean, he will be better soon, and I want to be gone."

"Have you got any leads on a new place? Do you have money for a deposit?"

"No."

"Tiffany, I'll help you as much as I can." Her mother had troubles of her own but hadn't said anything. She was still hoping things would turn around.

"I know, Mom. I'm trying to get more hours. I'm trying to make it."

"I'm proud of you, Tiffany. You are really taking control of things. I'm sure you will find a way."

Hearing those words from her mother made her feel better. She was determined to make a good life for herself and her children.

***

Joy arrived to work in a better mood. She was still upset with Tristan. More so because the conversation brought back bad memories. Having Brendan and the baby back at home helped her regain her peace. Brendan wasn't perfect, but she felt he was perfect for her. She didn't tell him about Tristan's visit, but she planned to. She felt she should also tell him about their relationship but felt that it wasn't the right time.

Her phone rang, breaking her train of thought.

"Hello."

"Joy, Tiffany wants to see you if you are not busy."

"Sure, send her in."

"Good morning, Tiffany. How can I help you today?"

Tiffany sank into a nearby chair and took a deep breath.

"Never mind," she said, standing to leave.

"Tiffany?"

"I need help," she blurted.

"What kind of help?"

Tiffany spent a few minutes telling Joy about the situation with Reggie and the police. She expressed her desire to move out of the apartment complex. Joy listened and let her talk.

"Tiffany, I have a house that will be completed this week. My properties are handled by Choice Realty."

"I don't have a deposit," Tiffany said, shaking her head.

"You can pay a little extra each month to make up that money. It's a small three bedroom and one and a half bath. If you are interested, here is the address. You can go look at it now. They are there painting. I can let them know you are coming. Also, I wanted to try training you for the desk because I have two people leaving soon. That will give you a bump in pay, plus guaranteed forty hours per week."

Tiffany was near tears. "Thank you," she said earnestly.

"Go on and look at it, and we can talk when you get back."

"Okay." She took the address and left. The house was only a few minutes from the hotel. The exterior was appealing.

Tiffany timidly knocked on the door. The painter let her in but cautioned her to be careful because of the wet walls. The house was very nice, and she was sure she could not afford it. She looked at the spacious eat-in kitchen and elegant formal dining room. There was also a sunporch. A sunporch was something she always wanted because she felt that it would be a good place for the children to play.

She walked through the rest of the rooms and found them all to be just as nice. *I'll never be able to afford this*, she said to herself and drove back to work. Later, Tiffany sat in the office and tried to contain herself. Joy was allowing her to rent the house at a rate lower than her current rent. This time, she let the tears fall. Things were definitely looking up.

Chapter 13

Ms. Plummer placed the phone back on its cradle. She sipped her tea and tried to calm down. She tried to persuade her lawyer into going forward with the case. Her lawyer refused. The lawyer informed her the case would be impossible to win. The conversation was short and to the point. However, it was long enough to infuriate her.

"Ms. Plummer, the father has established paternity. He did so before Vanessa's death. Vanessa's will also states she wants her daughter to be raised by her father in the case of her death," explained the lawyer. "Ms. Plummer, the child is not in any danger. She is living with her biological father."

"How do I know that?" snapped Ms. Plummer

"DNA testing was done at the hospital. His lawyer and I spoke today."

"He practically kidnapped my grandbaby. You can ask my other daughter; she was there."

"Ms. Plummer, she never lived with you. Her mother died, and now she's living with her father. You do not have a case."

"I will just contest the will then."

"Have a good day, Ms. Plummer."

She was looking forward to having that money. She sat in her easy chair mad enough to chew nails.

Carolyn walked into the room. "Momma, do you want a sandwich or something?"

"No!" she snapped.

"What's wrong with you? Do you need a pain pill?

"No, that was my lawyer. Talking 'bout I don't have a case," she said as she slammed down her empty teacup.

"Momma, were you really going to try and raise a baby?"

"She is my grandbaby; of course, I was."

"Momma, you just wanted the money," Carolyn said walking away.

"What did you say to me?"

"Momma, you never wanted the baby." Carolyn turned to face her. "You wanted nothing but Vanessa's money, Vanessa's houses, and Vanessa's car," she said slowly and clearly with emphasis on each word.

"Look, you better!" her mother started.

"Better what?!" she shouted as Ms. Plummer slowly rose and stood with the aid of her cane. Carolyn did not cower or back down. She stared defiantly at her mother. "What, Momma? I better what? Be quiet? Shut my mouth?" The anger and hurt Carolyn felt were evident in her voice. "That's what babies mean to you, isn't that right, momma? Money! Money! Money! Me and 'Nessa were just checks to you. Where is my child, Momma? Who did you sell it too?"

Shocked at the question, Ms. Plummer fell back into her chair. She opened and closed her mouth several times but was unable to speak.

"Please don't try to lie. I know what you did. That's how you got this house. You didn't just coincidentally get that money. Where is my child?"

"I did what I thought was best. I did what I thought was right at the time. We were barely making it. 'Nessa was in that expensive school. Then, you came up pregnant. How could I afford that alone? Your daddy's check wasn't that much, and with that money, we were able to move to a better place." Ms. Plummer began to cry.

Carolyn wasn't moved by her theatrics. She only wanted to know where to find her child. She reached down and grabbed her mother by the shoulders and demanded to know. Once she had forced the information out of her mother, she left her there to deal with her guilt.

***

Brendan and Joy received a call from the lawyer and were elated by the news. The case had been dropped. They celebrated by going out to dinner. Brenda gurgled and bounced happily as her parents enjoyed their meal.

"I'm glad that is over," Joy said.

"Yes, me too. I can't imagine life without my daughter. Ms. Plummer is her grandmother, but I don't trust her. You are a great mother to her; however, if anything should ever happen to me, there could be a problem. I want you to legally adopt Brenda. Getting married may not be enough."

"I never thought about that. Of course, I will. I love her like she is my own daughter. I'll look into it tomorrow."

"Thank you. It means a lot to me," Brendan said with a smile.

"Now that you will have to handle Vanessa's property, what are you going to do? If you choose to continue renting, the company I use is Choice Realty."

"Whoa! What property?" he asked.

"Well, I own some houses, and I rent them out."

"You do?"

"Yeah."

"Why haven't you told me about this before?"

"I don't know; I guess it never came up. It's not a big deal. I mean, I really don't think about it much. The realty company does all of the work. I get the funds direct deposited. As a matter of fact, Tiffany is moving into one of the houses next week."

"Tiffany who?"

"Your ex-wife, Brendan. She is having a hard time, so I gave her a good deal."

"She brought that on herself. Why didn't you say anything to me about it?"

"What is this? It just happened a few days ago. The subject never came up until now," Joy said defensively.

"Well, I hope you get your rent."

"Really Brendan?" she replied shocked at his attitude. "Look, I never asked you about your relationship with her. That's not my business. It's over and done with. Now, she's in need, and I was able to help, so I did."

"Okay, I was being petty. Hell, I never thought she would get a job, so maybe she has changed."

"I think it will be okay. So, let's get dessert," Joy said, changing the subject.

"Sure."

"Joy…" a faint voice called her name, and Joy turned abruptly at the sound of her name being called. When she turned, she accidentally knocked her water glass onto the floor. She was so busy trying to mop up the water that she missed Portia's second attempt to get her attention.

"What happened?" Brendan asked.

"Someone called my name. I don't see anyone, but I know someone called me." Joy turned and looked over her shoulder a few times without seeing a familiar face, so they finished dessert, paid, and left.

Portia was being escorted out of the restaurant by her husband. She followed him to the car bracing herself for the blows that were sure to come.

***

Brendan finally received the necessary paperwork from Vanessa's lawyer. He took time off to get the necessary changes made. He was now responsible for three houses and Vanessa's second car. He wasn't sure if he wanted to sell the car or not. He opened a bank account and included Brenda's name. He deposited all the funds he received from the various policies that Vanessa had. He decided to send fifty thousand each to Ms. Plummer and Carolyn. He felt it was a fair amount. With Joy's help, he was able to get Vanessa's house ready to rent.

"This is a lovely house," remarked Joy.

"Yeah."

"The nursery is simply beautiful."

"Yeah, it is."

Joy walked through the house and admired the newly painted rooms. Slim didn't want to be there. He didn't know why he felt so uncomfortable, but he did. The inspection went well, so they went home with Vanessa's second car in tow.

"Why are you so distant?" Joy asked.

"I just got a lot on my mind."

"Like what?"

"Well, I think I feel guilty."

"Why?"

"Vanessa."

"Brendan, her death was not your fault."

"Technically, it was not my fault, but if I hadn't gotten her pregnant she may still be alive," he said, shaking his head.

"You can't blame yourself. The fact is she was in town because she wanted to be, and you had nothing to do with it. Also, she didn't get pregnant alone. You both knew it was possible."

"She would not have had a reason to be in town had it not been for me."

Joy sighed and let the subject drop. It was times like this when she would have turned to Tristan or Portia. She never knew Slim felt that way. There was no need to continue with that conversation. She only hoped she would not be forced to compete with a ghost.

The week after they completed the inspection of Vanessa's house, Brendan finished moving in with Joy. He sold his unwanted furniture and also Vanessa's car. He used the money to purchase a new truck. The extra money from her insurance made him feel more confident. He didn't like the fact that Joy not only had more money than him but also made more money than him. It sometimes made him feel inadequate, but he never told her so. She never treated him as if it mattered, but it felt better now that he had some real money, as well.

Vanessa's death still weighed heavily on his conscience. He felt guilty, but he was grateful to be there to watch their child grow. Thanks to her financial planning, he would be able to do so without any financial strain.

Now that everything was in order, Joy only had one thing on her mind, the wedding. They just had about eight weeks left. Her mother was not happy about the wedding happening so soon. She felt Joy should have a much longer engagement. Her mother was also very concerned about her being taken advantage of and told her so. However, Joy was able to convince her she knew what she was doing. With a little more push back, she finally relented. With the task of planning a wedding, she made every day count. Joy had full confidence in her mother and didn't worry. She was only concerned about the growing number of guests.

"Mom, this is my second wedding. It should be small and intimate."

"Yes, but just a few more folks won't hurt."

"Mom…"

"Okay, okay."

"I want to enjoy my family, not entertain strangers."

"Jocelyn."

"Mother."

They both laughed.

"Okay honey, I understand, and I'm just so happy you let me do this."

"Well, Mom, I'm sure you know what you're doing."

"I appreciate that."

"See you soon, Mom."

"Bye, baby."

Joy sat back in her office chair and relaxed. Moving Tiffany up to desk clerk was turning out to be a good thing. She was eager to learn and easy to train. She was still a little rough around the edges but overall a good desk agent. If things continued to go well with her, she was seriously considering making her the new assistant.

She believed promoting from within would be better, and Tiffany wanted to work. Whatever she asked her to do got done in a timely manner. The slow season had begun, so the housekeeping department was slowing down. She was able to move a room attendant to the laundry position. She had all of her bases covered for right now. Things were finally settling down, or so she thought.

Chapter 14

Walt hadn't gotten up the nerve to go and see his son. He and his wife were enjoying their marriage for the first time. He realized all the time he wasted on outside relationships he could have devoted to his wife. They spent time talking and getting to know each other. He chastened himself for losing so much time. Now they enjoyed each day to the fullest.

Seeing her truly happy made it hard for him to express his feelings. Now that he knew about his son, he wanted to meet him. After all the years of affairs and lies, he wanted to do things right. He had to meet his son with her blessing. The pain was still there for her, but he needed to know his child. This was his only child who was now a grown man. He was a grown man who probably had children of his own.

Walt quietly walked into their bedroom. His wife was relaxing in the chaise lounge watching TV.

"Belle."

"Yes, dear?"

"I want to meet my son."

"We are finally happy together. We finally have a real marriage."

"He is my son, Belle."

"I know, but what about his mother?"

"Belle, I am no longer in love with Claire. I love you. I just want to meet my son."

She sighed. "I understand."

"You can come along if it will make you feel better."

"No, I don't think I want to see the child you had with some other woman."

Understanding her pain, he pulled her into his arms. All he could do was hold her. He could not turn back the hands of time or erase the past.

"I'm so sorry, really I am. Please understand that I need to see my child. I'm not going to see her. I was wrong, and I admit it. Regardless of how our marriage started, we were married, and I did not respect that. I'm sorry truly, but please let me meet my son."

"Okay, Walt, I understand that you're right."

"Thank you." He scooped her up into his arms and settled on the chair with her.

***

Claire decided to drive up to Sam's for her monthly supplies. She finished her shopping and dropped by the hotel to speak with her soon to be daughter-in-law. Nothing she had was perishable and, hopefully, her daughter-in-law would be up to going to lunch. Her favorite restaurant was actually next door. She parked close to the door and walked into the lobby.

"Hi, Ms. McNair."

"Tiffany?"

"Yes ma'am, how can I help you?"

"I came to see Joy."

"Sure, I will buzz her for you."

Once inside Joy's office, the look on her face said it all.

"Yes ma'am, she works here," Joy acknowledged.

"And how is that going?"

"She is actually really good."

"Okay, if you say so. I just wanted to say hi and take my favorite daughter to lunch."

"Sure! Let's go."

Joy knew without asking that her mother-in-law wanted to go to the restaurant next door, so she reached under her desk and slid on her flats. Joy let Tiffany know she was headed out for lunch, and the two ladies headed out.

Claire wanted to ask more about Tiffany but decided to let the subject drop even though she was very concerned about Tiffany working so closely with Joy. She knew Tiffany made her way through life by using other people. She was surprised to see she was actually holding down a job. Throughout her short marriage to her son, she barely worked. Maybe she had changed. However, Claire felt it was necessary to warn Joy to keep an eye on her.

The two ladies enjoyed lunch and conversation. Joy filled her in on the wedding plans and the baby's progress. The discussion was going great until Claire froze mid-sentence.

"Ms. McNair, are you okay? You look like you've seen a ghost."

"I think I just did."

"Are you okay?"

"Yes, I think I better go and let you get back to work."

"Are you sure?"

"Yes, I need to go back. I have a bit of a drive, you know."

"You can stay with us tonight if you need to. We would love to have you."

"No, I have things I need to do at home."

"Okay," Joy said.

Claire hugged Joy then headed to her car. She watched Joy walk into the hotel as she walked hurriedly to her car and pressed the auto unlock on her keychain. She'd just placed her hand on her door handle when she heard her name being called.

"Claire?" She recognized the voice immediately and did not want to turn around. She almost got in her car and drove away, but instead, she turned and faced him.

"Hello, Walt."

"It's been a long time, Claire."

"Yes, it has. It's been almost forty years."

"I'm here to meet my son."

"How did you find us? He doesn't know about you, Walt. I got your message."

"What are you talking about, Claire?"

"Your wife came to my job; you know the one you never told me about? She came to confront me. I was shocked, to say the least. I told her we were expecting a baby and I had no idea you were married. A few days later, a messenger brought me a package with a check for ten thousand dollars and a note telling me you had decided to end our affair. You didn't want anything to do with me or the baby because your wife and family would not understand. You said you never wanted to see me again. I was devastated, to say the least."

"Claire, I thought you were dead."

"Why? Why would you think that? I called you and told you I was pregnant. You said you were going to meet me and never showed up."

"My wife showed me a newspaper article that said you were killed in a car crash at the time. I didn't know she knew about you or that she had spoken to you. I believed her and grieved for years for you and the child. My brother met your son a few weeks ago by chance. That's why I'm here to meet my son. I didn't know you two were alive, or I would have been here. I would never have left you like that. I loved you."

She looked into his eyes and realized he was telling the truth.

"All this time I thought you didn't want us. I never told him your name or anything about us. I just raised him the best that I could."

"For that, I apologize. Now, all I want is to know my son."

"I understand."

Seeing her again brought back memories but no feelings. She had been dead to him for too long. He smiled and said, "You are just as beautiful as the last time I saw you."

"Thank you, Walt."

They spent a few minutes talking. Claire gave him directions to Brendan's house then left for home. Walt was just as dashing as he was forty years ago, but she didn't say so. She was no longer a sixteen-year-old schoolgirl in love. Knowing he would have been there erased some of the anger. She also realized had she been in his wife's place she may have done the same thing. However, she did feel angry because her child grew up without a father because of a lie. She felt like a coward driving home knowing she should be there when Brendan met his father, but she needed to work through her own emotions.

***

Joy came home and found the house was empty. She kicked off her shoes and changed into sweats. While walking down the hall, she thought she heard voices. She was walking to the living room and saw Brendan outside on the patio. He had the grill going, and the baby was playing nearby and her portable playpen. She's slid open the door and realized they had company.

"Hello, Mr. Walt. How are you?"

He looked up at her and recognition made him smile.

"Girl, you look good!"

"Thanks."

"So, you are marrying my son."

"Yes, in a matter of weeks. I hope you can make it to the wedding."

"I will try my best."

"I'll take over diaper duty. You two guys have a lot of catching up to do." Joy took the baby and went inside. She was happy to see them together. She was glad things were working out for Brendan and the void of not having his father in his life was being filled. Happiness was all she saw on both faces. When she found out Walt was staying in her hotel, she wondered if he had seen Claire. She didn't want to ask, but something told her that he had. She was curious about their relationship and why Claire never told Brendan anything about his father. Not even his name.

All through dinner, she wanted to ask but never could bring herself to do so. She enjoyed the evening with Walt and Brendan and was pleased to know Walt would be in town for the weekend. After dinner was over, she was putting away leftovers when it suddenly hit her.

Slim and the Lady

Claire had seen him in the restaurant. That was the ghost she saw.

Later that night, Brendan fell into bed and pulled his lady into his arms. He told her about the plans he and his father had made. He filled her in on all he had learned about his father. Joy snuggled, smiled, and listened.

***

Tristan decided to make a quick run to a local Wal-Mart. The last few days had been hectic, and he was dangerously low on most of his household items. Wal-Mart was close and always open, which made it his usual choice. He grabbed the cart and started down the aisle. He remembered he needed mouthwash, so he headed in that direction. He turned down the aisle and was pleasantly surprised to see his Uncle Walt.

"Looking for something, old man?"

"Hey there!"

"Uncle Walt, what are you doing here?"

"I came here to meet my son," he stated proudly.

"Your what?"

"Yep, I have a son. He took out the grill and made barbecue today, and now I need some Pepto- Bismol. An old man like me can't eat all that pork."

"Well, does he stay close by here?"

"Yeah, real close. He stays in that subdivision, something Estates."

"Holland Estates?"

"Yeah, that's it."

"Well, he is doing well for himself then. That's a nice subdivision. I don't stay too far from there myself."

"And guess what nephew?"

"What?"

"He is marrying Joy. The same little girl you used to hang with all the time."

"Say that again."

"Yeah, she turned out to be quite a looker. Hey, they are having dinner tomorrow. Why don't you come with me?"

"I don't know about that."

"Awe, come on. You and Joy grew up together. Plus, that's your first cousin, and he needs to know his family."

Seeing an advantage in the situation, Tristan changed his mind.

"Okay, I'll be there. Wait, why don't we go together?"

"Okay, that's a great idea."

Tristan smiled as he thought about the upcoming dinner. He knew Joy would not throw him out in front of Walt. He finished picking up his items and chatted with his uncle all the while thinking, *all is fair in Love and War.*

***

Joy dressed for dinner. She wanted to look nice for her soon-to-be father-in-law. She put a cute pink dress on the baby, as well. She was looking forward to Walt's visit. Brendan was happy to know his father, and she loved seeing him this way. His happiness was infectious. She was almost floating herself until she answered the door.

"Look who I bumped into last night," Walt said while smiling from ear-to-ear.

"Hi, Tristan. You two come on in," she said with a fake smile. Brendan didn't fake anything. Joy recognized the danger signs and walked over to him and placed her arm around his waist. "Your dad wants you to meet your cousin, Tristan."

"We've met," he responded.

Joy gave Tristan a warning look, which he ignored. She knew Tristan had something up his sleeve. She tried her best to keep the two men apart throughout dinner. She would change the subject when possible to keep the conversation light. When dinner was finally over, she excused herself to put the baby down. The men went outside to the patio to enjoy the nice weather and talk. Joy cleared the dishes and began loading the dishwasher.

"So, scamming you wasn't enough," the sound of Tristan's voice startled her.

"What are you talking about, Tristan?"

"Him, Joy. He has scammed his way into your house, and now he's trying to take my uncle."

"Tristan, you don't know what you are talking about. Brendan didn't scam anyone."

"Really? My uncle is filthy rich, never had a child, and then all of a sudden he shows up out of nowhere?"

"Tristan, leave. I'm not going to entertain this nonsense."

"Why are you marrying him? Do you have a prenup?"

"Tristan, none of this is your business. I'm asking you again to please leave."

"No, you don't know him. You could lose everything."

"Tristan, please don't do this."

"And where did this baby come from? Where is her mother? That is not your child. You have only had one child, my child. Does he even know about T.J.?"

"Who is T.J.?" asked Brendan as he walked into the kitchen.

The sound of his voice made Joy jump. Brendan stood in the doorway holding two empty glasses.

"Brendan, not now," she pleaded

"No, I want to know," Brendan said as he walked further into the kitchen.

"Tell him, Joy," Tristan demanded.

"Hey, did the party move to the kitchen?" Walt walked in holding his empty glass.

Breathing a sigh of relief, Joy walked past the two angry men, took Walt's glass and refilled it.

"Uncle Walt, they left you outside alone? Come on into the living room and relax." She glanced back at the two men and added, "Boys, the party has moved to the living room."

Chapter 15

Tiffany moved into her new house and quickly unpacked. She didn't have much furniture, but what she had was carefully arranged and clean. She was proud of her new place. Each of her children had their own room. The house was more spacious, and the sunporch was used as a play area for the children. Since she no longer lived next door to Ms. Murphy, she had to secure a sitter. Luckily, there was a reasonably-priced, home-based daycare a few houses down. She was lucky enough to get the last two spaces available. She hadn't heard from Reggie, but she knew he was out of the hospital. She did not know who he was living with and didn't care. Her children were her top priority. Once she was satisfied everything was in its proper place, she put the children down for a nap. As soon as she got settled on the sofa, there was a knock at the door. She cautiously looked through the peephole.

"Momma!" she exclaimed happily.

"Hey, baby, take this."

"Thanks, Mom," she said while looking at the new kitchen towels.

"This is beautiful. Are you sure you can afford this?"

"Yes, I got it, Mom."

"I'm so proud of you, Tiffany. You have really turned things around."

"Thanks, Mom."

Her mom took a tour of the new house. "Girl, this is a real nice place."

"I know, Mom; I got a really great deal."

"You told me your landlord is your boss, right?"

"Yeah, Joy."

"She must really like you then."

"She's really nice, but…"

"But what? What's wrong?"

"She is Slim's fiancée."

"What did you just say?"

"Yeah, my boss is my ex-husband's fiancée."

"How are you dealing with that?"

"Mom, when I found out, I was so hurt, but I needed that job. I'm so glad I stayed."

"You never told me that, Tiffany."

"Well, I really didn't know how to tell you. The same day I found out she was his fiancée is the same day I met his baby's Momma."

"He has a baby? Does your boss know that you're his ex-wife?"

"Yeah, she knows and, yes, he has a baby."

"And she's okay with it?"

"Yeah, obviously, 'cause she's been nothing but nice to me, and at work, she's very professional."

"Well, that's good. I just hope things don't get ugly."

"So far so good," Tiffany said.

"Yeah, but you never know. Just be careful," her mother warned.

"I will, Momma."

Tiffany hoped her luck would last.

***

Tiffany's new position was challenging, but she was not backing down. Desk clerks routinely had to complete hour-long courses online. The classes were designed to improve performance and customer service. If any new procedures were being implemented, they would be outlined in the classes as well. Being new to the front desk, Tiffany had quite a few to complete. She carefully followed the instructions in the manual and was able to successfully complete her assigned tasks. She felt good about her recent accomplishments. The new system was a challenge to all of the clerks, but she was mastering it faster than all the other desk agents, mainly because she was determined to excel.

Joy needed an assistant, and Tiffany wanted the position. Even though she was a new hire, the odds were in her favor. Her only concern was Brittany. Brittany had been with the company for years and often used her seniority to get her way. Tiffany didn't feel she was a big threat because most of her morning was spent correcting the mistakes Brittany had made the day before.

Tiffany's new position gave her the means to take care of herself and her children. If she could get the promotion, she wouldn't need any outside assistance. That was her goal. She wanted to become totally independent and make sure she would be able to continue to afford her new and improved living conditions. She arrived to work early every morning and made sure her uniform was immaculate. She had learned her lesson and would not go back to depending upon anyone for her needs.

Reggie had started calling, so she changed her phone number. She knew she couldn't hide from him forever. The restraining order meant nothing to him. He knew where she worked, so it was just a matter of time. The only thing she could do was deal with it when it happened. She was not going to run from him.

With only fifteen minutes left in her shift, she cleared the counter and made sure all of the end of the day paperwork was done. Her relief walked in smacking a wad of gum and snapping her fingers. Tiffany glanced at her long enough to give a quick smile. She patiently waited on her to put down all of her bags and count down the register.

"This cash drawer is short," Brittany snapped.

Tiffany handed her the drop sheet.

"It is still short."

"Brittany, you have to add my drops and subtract my withdrawals," Tiffany replied calmly.

"Why can't you just make sure it's right before I get here?"

"It is right, Brittany," she replied, getting agitated. Every day it was the same thing. Brittany could not handle the smallest task without it being explained to her several times. Tiffany leaned against the desk and waited.

Brittany dropped the till back into the drawer and closed it. She turned and headed towards the manager's office.

"Joy, my drawer is short again. Every time she works, my money is wrong," she shouted to make sure Tiffany heard her.

Joy walked out to the desk and asked her to count down the drawer. Brittany counted the money again.

"See, it's short."

Joy picked up the drop sheet and asked, "Did you add the drops and subtract the withdrawals?"

"No, it is supposed to be…"

Joy raised her hand to silence her.

"Brittany, you have been here longer than any other clerk. I should not have to explain this to you. It is simple as adding and subtracting. Your drawer is correct." She turned to Tiffany and said, "You can clock out." Joy shook her head and walked away. The exasperated look on her face made Tiffany smile inwardly.

Tiffany gathered her things and left without a word. It was just a matter of time, but that position was going to be hers.

Chapter 16

Tristan felt remorseful on the way home. He intended to ruin the evening until he saw how happy she was. Still, he had to know why she was so intent upon marrying that man. At first, he was certain Brendan was out to get her money. Now, he wasn't so sure. He seemed to really love her. Tristan was later surprised when his uncle told him about his affair that resulted in his birth.

"Yeah, almost forty years ago, I met this cute little lady at a fast food joint. She was the sweetest little thing, and I fell hard for her."

"Why didn't you marry her?" Tristan asked.

"Well, first off, I was already married. Secondly, she was only sixteen. And no, I didn't know she was that young."

"What happened? Did she hide the pregnancy from you? Or did you just decide to work it out with Aunt Belle?"

"No, I knew she was pregnant. What I didn't know was that your aunt knew about it. She led me to believe that Claire had died in a car crash. She had a fake news page and everything. I grieved for years. Your uncle James ran into Brendan, and he looked so much like a young me that he struck up a conversation with him."

"Wow. So, if Uncle James hadn't run into him, you two may not have met."

"Yeah, I never would have known."

"Wonder why he never looked for you."

"His mother never told him my name," he replied sadly.

"So, how is Aunt Belle taking it? I mean, you been here a few days."

"It still bothers her. But we are really working on our relationship."

"Well, that's good," Tristan said.

"So tell me, nephew, how long have you been in love with Joy?"

Tristan was caught off guard by his uncle's question. He had no idea it was obvious. It took almost a full minute for him to reply, "Since college."

"Didn't you two date for a while?" his uncle asked.

"Yeah, we did."

"How serious was it?"

"Very."

"Very?" repeated his uncle.

"We had a baby."

"What?"

"He died in his sleep. SIDS was the official cause of death, but she blamed me."

"Why didn't I know about this?"

"I didn't know right away myself. When she told me, she was already about halfway through the pregnancy. She kept going to class until the last week. She told her mother when she was in the hospital."

"Why does she blame you for his death?"

"He was at my apartment that night. I woke up, and he was cold."

"I'm sorry."

"Thanks, Uncle Walt."

They rode the rest of the way in silence. Each man was lost in thought. Tristan thought about what had just transpired. If she ever forgave him, their friendship would never be the same. He only brought up the baby to hurt her. He knew that was a trigger. He felt awful. His behavior was petty and childish. Maybe it was time to let the friendship go. It was hard being just friends with a woman he was in love with.

Walt knew his wife would have hundreds of questions when he returned. He wanted to develop a relationship with his son. He and Brendan discussed meeting monthly. Now that he and his wife were trying to have a real relationship, he didn't want to cause yet another rift. He wanted to have a relationship with his son with her blessing. If only she would understand.

***

Joy finished the kitchen and locked the patio door. She fluffed the pillows and turned out the lights. There wasn't anything left to do, so she had to face him. She walked into the bedroom, sat on the settee, and removed her shoes. Brendan was sitting across from her in the easy chair. He looked at her and waited. When she spoke, it was just above a whisper.

"T.J. was my son."

"Was?"

"He died in infancy."

"Who was his father?" he asked but only for confirmation. He already knew what she was about to say.

"Tristan," she stated and looked him in the eye. He ignored her pleading eyes.

Brendan stood and walked out of the room. Joy watched him leave.

For two days, they barely spoke to each other. He refused to acknowledge her presence when she walked in a room, and he didn't sleep in their room. They only spoke to each other when necessary. On the third day, Joy had had enough. She was tired of him walking past her in the hallway as if she were invisible. She understood that he was upset, but he was taking things too far.

"Brendan, we need to talk."

"So, you want to talk now?"

"That's not fair, Brendan."

"You said you two were just friends. Then, you said you dated in college, not that you two had a child together. You lied to me."

"You have every right to be upset, but I did not lie. I omitted some things because I did not know how to tell you."

"Were you ever going to tell me?" he asked.

"Honestly, I don't know. I try not to think about it. I should have been upfront. I should have told you that day in the car. I'm sorry, Brendan. I demanded you be upfront with me, and I had secrets."

"You're right. If we are going to make this thing work then we have to be honest and upfront with each other." He reached for her. "I'm sorry for how I acted or reacted. Maybe I should not have taken it this far. I'm sorry for your loss. I know that had to be hard."

She walked into his arms and let him hold her.

"Are we okay?" she asked, looking up at him.

He wiped the tears from her eyes and nodded yes. Slowly and tenderly, he kissed her and pulled her closer. They stood in the hallway and held each other.

"Joy, I love you so much."

"I love you too, and I should have told you."

"Well, I know now, so he doesn't have anything else to hold over my head. Or does he?"

"No."

"Let's hurry and put the baby to bed so that we can get to bed. We have some making up to do."

"Yes we do," she said with a smile.

Chapter 17

Carolyn put the majority of her new wealth in the bank. She used some of the money to purchase a new car. Her mother was not at all satisfied with that 'little bit of change.' However, she was spending it like water.

The relationship between mother and daughter was beyond strained. After her mother finally gave her the information she needed, Carolyn hadn't spoken more than a few words to her. She wanted to call Brendan, but she did not know how to break the news to him. It had been twenty-three years since that summer, but he needed to know they had a child. After the birth, she was angry. She thought she would never see her child or him again. Seeing him at the hospital was definitely a shock. Never in a million years would she have thought the man Vanessa referred to as 'Slim' was Brendan McNair.

Now that she knew her child's whereabouts, she was ready to go. Carolyn was packing and getting things ready for her trip. She wanted to leave as early as possible. She was getting ready to fuel the car when she remembered she had the money to fly. She called the airline and purchased a ticket.

Carolyn drove to the airport and parked. Her flight was due to leave in an hour. She grabbed her bag, checked in, and waited. Her eyes wandered around the room. She noticed a young mother nearby trying to entertain her small child. The child who was unaware of her limitations tried to pull away. After several attempts, the mother let go, and the child fell with a noisy plop.

Carolyn couldn't help smiling. Moments like those were precious. She missed all of her child's precious moments. Time was one thing she would never get back. All of these years, she wanted to know what happened to her child. She didn't know if she was dead or alive. She couldn't believe her child had been raised by her aunt without her knowledge.

Carolyn's aunt was pregnant that same summer. Being in her mid-forties, she was never expected to have children. Her aunt was ecstatic and telling anyone that would listen. There were two things Carolyn didn't know; one was that her aunt had lost her baby late in the pregnancy, and the other was that her aunt knew of her pregnancy. When her aunt lost her own child, she asked her sister to let her raise Carolyn's baby. When her mother finally confessed, she called it a blessing in disguise. The two sisters had hatched a plan that directly affected her without her knowledge or permission.

Carolyn signed the car rental agreement and collected her keys. She drove straight to her aunt's house.

Even though it had been several years since she'd visited, she knew the way. Soon, the large, plantation-style house was visible. She pulled into the driveway and took a few minutes to collect herself. She turned her head and surveyed the large lawn. The hedges were neat and the yard immaculate. She always loved spending summers there when she was a little girl. She got out of the car and walked up to the front door. She rang the doorbell and waited.

"I've been expecting you. Your mother called me and told me you were coming up," her aunt said with a smile.

"Where is she?" Carolyn asked.

"She isn't here now, but she will be here tonight."

"What time should I come back?"

"Around seven."

"Okay." Carolyn turned to walk out.

"Wait. Can you stay with me tonight?"

"For what?"

"Carolyn, please don't be angry with me. I'm so sorry. I wanted to tell you. But your mother felt you would be better off not knowing."

"She was my baby. How would you feel if someone took your child? You could have asked me. Me. Her mother. I know we couldn't afford her. I may have felt better about it had I just known. Can you imagine wondering for years where your child is? I was wondering if she was dead or alive only to find out she was within reach the entire time."

"I'm so sorry, Carolyn."

"Does she know about me?"

"No."

"How long were you two planning on telling this lie?"

"I don't know."

Carolyn wanted to throw something.

"Vivian will be staying the night. Please stay with us."

"I have a hotel room in town."

"Cancel it and stay with us. I want to tell her tonight."

Carolyn conceded. She called and canceled her room. "Okay, it's done. Where do I sleep tonight?"

"Come on. I'll show you to your room."

Carolyn followed her aunt to the top of the stairs. She couldn't help but notice the beautiful decor. "Where is her room? I want to see how my little girl grew up," she said.

"This way." Her aunt opened the door to a large, airy room.

Carolyn stood just inside the doorway and surveyed the room. "I never could have given her this." She turned and faced her aunt. She wasn't angry anymore; she was grateful. "Thank you."

Vivian pulled into the driveway. She parked next to Carolyn's compact rental car. She wondered who was visiting. Since her father died, her mother didn't go out much but often had company. She just hoped it wasn't one of those gossiping old ladies from the church. She grabbed her bags and headed up the walk.

"Mom, I'm home," she shouted as she walked through the door.

"Girl, you are going to wake the dead."

"Who's here?" she asked as she walked through the front door.

"Can I get a hug before I have to answer questions?" She hugged her mother and planted a loud smack on her cheek. "You silly, girl."

"Come on in the kitchen I need to talk to you."

Minutes later, Vivian sat in the chair completely still. She was absolutely dumbstruck. Adopted? How could she be adopted? Her parents were older than most, but she looked just like her mother in her opinion. Who were her real parents? She looked up at her mother. She sat silently across from her dabbing the corners of her eyes.

"Do you have any idea who my parents are?" asked Vivian.

Her mother wiped her eyes and cleared her throat. She dropped her head.

"Mom, I just want to know. You will always be my mom. Nothing can change that."

Her mother looked into her eyes and said, "My sister's baby girl got in trouble when she was fifteen."

Vivian slowly digested the information. "Cousin Carolyn is my birth mother? Then, who is my father?"

"I don't know, baby. I'm sorry I didn't tell you sooner. I was so happy to have you. It was not my intention to deceive you."

"Why did she give me away?

"She didn't have a choice."

"Why didn't she say anything."

"I didn't know," Carolyn replied, walking into the kitchen. "My mother made me sign the adoption papers, and I had no idea that Auntie had you. I didn't know where you were."

Vivian saw the hurt in Carolyn's eyes. She stood and walked over to her and hugged her with all her might. Vivian insisted on Carolyn staying in her room. She wanted to know as much as she could about her. They talked, laughed, and cried late into the night. She knew Vivian would want to know about her father. It was only natural that she would. She didn't want to have to explain to her that she had a sister that was also her cousin. She didn't want Vivian to have a negative view of her father. There was no way to let her know who her father was without telling her. She would change the subject whenever she felt the conversation leading that way.

Vivian decided not to play that game. She just came out and asked, "Who is my father?"

"My first love," Carolyn answered.

"Can you tell me about it?"

"Give me some time, and I will."

"Okay," Vivian responded.

Carolyn pulled her daughter into her arms and held her. They made plans to go shopping and get pedicures the next day. Carolyn was more than happy to oblige. They crammed as much as they could into the two days that followed. They shopped, talked, and ate. They did not leave each other until it was time for Carolyn to fly back. They made plans to get together again in a few weeks. Carolyn had to tell Brendan, and a phone call just didn't feel right. It had to be in person.

Chapter 18

Portia sat soaking in the large tub. She let the water and Epsom salt do its job. She was tired of her new life but couldn't find a way out. She didn't have access to money like she thought she would. He said she didn't need any, so she spent most of her time indoors; sometimes, she would walk the grounds. The life she imagined was just a fantasy, and now reality was hitting her in the face literally.

She was so happy to see a familiar face at the restaurant that she yelled out her name without thinking. Her husband didn't cause a scene, but she knew the situation could escalate quickly. He ushered her out of the restaurant. She had only a moment to glance back and see Joy's happiness.

The steam from the bath was soothing. She slid further down in the tub resting her head on her foam pillow. Tears slowly ran down her cheeks. She sat there thinking she had all the things she deserved to have, but none of them brought the comfort she expected. She thought of the irony of lying in a large Jacuzzi tub only to soak away soreness. In her fantasy, it was to have romantic baths and make love to her husband. She had closets full of designer clothes but nowhere to wear them. The huge kitchen she always wanted was meticulously kept and void of smell. It was so sterile looking that it gave her the creeps.

She wished she had her friend. She understood what Joy meant now. She was not happy but had everything she thought she wanted. Joy was right. She was marrying for money. She didn't love him, only what she thought he would give her. One thing she knew for sure was true happiness couldn't be bought.

A few days later, Portia was ready to jump from a window. She was holding a cold compress to her head, hoping the swelling wouldn't be too bad. He was becoming more violent. Evidently, there was an issue at work. She overheard him yelling about some missing money, and she was now afraid for her life. More and more, he was taking his frustrations out on her. She heard him enter her room. She turned and faced him but did not speak.

"I'm sorry, sweetheart," he said in a soft, almost loving voice. He took the cold compress from her and kissed her forehead. "Can we talk?"

She looked at him trying to gauge his mood.

"Baby, I do love you. I should never have put my hands on you unless it was to hold you. I am going to counseling because I want to do better. Can we try to work things out?"

She was confused by his admission of guilt and wanted desperately to believe his words were genuine. Something told her not to believe him. He was a convincing liar; otherwise, she wouldn't be married to him. She smiled and nodded her head because she didn't trust her voice. It may give her away.

He pulled her up into a standing position and helped her over to the bed. "You need some rest. I'll check on you tomorrow. Maybe take you shopping, okay?"

Again, she nodded and watched him walk out of the room. She had to plan her escape. She realized now that there were red flags from the beginning. However, her desire to marry a rich man blinded her and clouded her judgment.

That night, before she fell asleep, she prayed. She cried out to the Lord and begged for forgiveness. She asked the Lord to deliver her from her situation. He was the only one she could turn to. As she fell asleep, she could hear her grandmother say, 'When life knocks you down go ahead and pray and when you get up pray some more.'

Portia went through her days cautiously. Her husband had been very attentive and almost as affectionate as when they were dating. However, she lived in fear and trepidation. Recently, he was more lenient as well, taking her out, even having the driver to take her shopping. She planned to leave during one of these rare occasions. Portia felt good about her plan until she woke up sick and realized she was pregnant.

Portia wasn't sure how her husband would react to the news of her pregnancy. With all the drama in her life, she missed the fact that her body was trying to tell her something. Under different circumstances, she would have been ecstatic. If she was to leave now, how would she take care of herself and a child? She had quit her job after becoming engaged and sold her condo. She was dependent upon her husband for everything.

Weighing the pros and cons, she felt staying would be the best decision. She did not love him, but until she could do better, she would have to stay. He hadn't laid a hand on her in anger in over two weeks. Maybe the baby would bring about a change.

"Hello! Is anybody home?" he called out.

"Yes, I'm upstairs in my room."

"Have you been in bed all day? You are still in pajamas."

"Mostly. I need to see a doctor."

"Why? What's wrong? Are you in pain?"

"No, I believe that I'm pregnant."

"Get dressed. Let's go to the drug store and pick up a test." His exuberant behavior caused her mood to lighten as well.

Maybe things will get better, she hoped. She hurriedly dressed, and they drove to the store. She was almost giddy while trying to find the right test. They chose one and rushed back home.

The results were positive, and he couldn't contain his joy. That night, she slept in the room with him. Before falling asleep, she prayed he would stay this way.

Chapter 19

Reggie sat in the wheelchair and waited. In the end, his mother was the only person he had to lean on. When she finally showed up, she helped him into the car. He moaned when he felt a sharp pain when trying to get comfortable in the seat. Once she had him settled in the car, she placed his wheelchair in the trunk. Reggie sat silently in the passenger seat. He knew he would get an earful on the way home. He avoided calling his mother for that very reason.

"So, now, what are you going to do, Reggie?"

"What do you mean, Mom?"

"Have you filed for short-term disability or anything?"

"I did that before I left the hospital, but you know that does not mean I will get it."

"Well, you better find something because this is only temporary."

"I just got out of the hospital. Can I at least have a few days?"

"No, you cannot. You been out the house long enough to have established yourself instead of making babies all over town. Hell, if I was your wife, I would have shot your ass too."

Reggie took the verbal abuse for two main reasons. One, she was his mother, and two, she was right. He was close to thirty and did not have a dime. It was humiliating sitting in the car with his mother yelling at him like he was still a kid.

But again, she was right. His wife was gone, and no one knew where. He had no idea where any of his children were. He had to reevaluate his life. He could have been dead or in the chair for the rest of his life. She missed permanently paralyzing him by less than an inch. He was lucky. He was not raised to be in and out of jail. However, the longest he held down a job after high school was a year.

His mother continued to yell at him all the way home. He stayed silent. The past few years were spent bed hopping and living off women. He was a grown man behaving like a spoiled child.

"Well, the doctor said you will need an additional few weeks at least, so during that time you will be online and looking through the paper to see what you can do. I'm tired of you telling me what you can't do. You don't have any felonies on your record, so you should be able to find something."

"Yes, ma'am," he said and leaned back in the chair in an attempt to get more comfortable. He turned his head and watched the scenery quickly pass by. He realized his life was like the scenery. It was time to stop letting life pass him by and make things right.

The weeks spent at his mother's house gave him time to recuperate and land a job. There was a new call center opening up, and he had applied. Like all the other applications, he only applied to make his mother happy. Reggie never thought he would get an interview, let alone a job.

Before he could ask, his father gave him a used car and secured a small one bedroom apartment for him to live in. He took them with the understanding that he would have to pay his father back.

His mother helped him improve his meager wardrobe and helped him furnish his apartment. He also became familiar with the thrift store.

He felt like things were finally falling into place for him. He had gone by the hotel a few times, but Tiffany wasn't there. He had no idea how to find her, and her coworkers were of no help. For now, he decided to concentrate on getting himself together.

The women really meant nothing to him. All he wanted was to at least have a chance to see his children regularly. Tiffany was just an affair, just like she was in high school. He didn't feel guilty at all about the relationship but did feel like he should have been a better father to his children. Contrary to popular belief, he loved his children—all of them.

Reggie knew he needed money to do anything about it. Now that he had a job, he was going to make things happen.

***

Tiffany smiled so hard her face began to hurt. Joy had offered her the position. Training would start in a week. She was being sent to another property to train. She excitedly dialed her mother's phone number.

"Mom, guess what?!" she almost shouted into the phone.

"What's up, Tip?

"I got the promotion."

"Congratulations, baby."

"Thanks, Momma. I was calling to see if you could take care of the kids for me for a few days."

"Why, what's wrong?"

"I have to go out of town to train."

"Okay, when?"

"What's wrong, Mom?" she asked once she finally noticed the flat sounding responses.

"Tip, not now."

"Momma, what is all that noise?"

Her mother let out a sigh and said, "I got evicted."

"What? What happened?"

"Well, they kept cutting back hours and finally laid us off for a few weeks. Then, when I went back, I only had about twenty or thirty hours. I couldn't keep up the payments."

"What are you planning to do, Mom?"

"First, I sold off what I could. I have been trying to get a better job, but nothing has come through."

"Momma, come stay with me until you get on your feet."

"I don't want to do that."

"Well, where are you going to go? Your boyfriend can't help. Big Ma lives all the way in the country, and you know you don't want to go there."

"You're right, Tiffany. Give me a few days to clear up things here, and I will be over— temporarily."

"Mom, you are more than welcome."

Tiffany felt good about her decision and smiled thinking about the free childcare she would have for a while. She could almost count the dollars she would save by letting her mom move in. Childcare was one of her largest expenditures. It only took a few days for her to realize she had made a horrible mistake.

Tiffany returned from training with more confidence. Her new title meant she would be in charge while Joy was gone. Everything was checked and rechecked. She wanted to make sure all the supplies were plentiful and well-stocked. She personally inventoried the supply room and cart rooms. Taking the initiative would show her leadership capabilities. She had the job as an assistant and wanted to keep it.

Now that her career was on track, her home life was falling apart. Her mother was more of a nuisance than a help. Tiffany came home early to find her mother's fat, lazy boyfriend sitting on her sofa in his drawers, and he had left a trail of mess from the kitchen to the sofa. When she spoke to her mother about it, she had the nerve to have an attitude with her. She ended up giving her mother an ultimatum.

"Well, I said *you* could stay here until you get on your feet."

"So, since you got this new house, you think you all that," her mother said.

"Momma, you know that you're wrong. I offered a place for you to stay rent-free. All I ask you to do was watch my children. I came home to your man in his drawers on my couch and my kids locked out on the sunporch both wet and crying."

Her mother could only stand there and look embarrassed.

"You're right; I was wrong for having him here."

"Mom, I'm sorry, but you got a month."

"What will you do for a babysitter?"

"I'll figure it out."

Her mother wanted to say more, but she knew Tiffany was right. She should have had more respect for her. She was taking advantage. She gave her daughter a curt nod and said, "Okay, Tiffany, thirty days."

Chapter 20

Carolyn cleaned and re-cleaned her spare room. She added new curtains and bedding. The comforter set cost more than anything she owned. She wanted the best for her baby. Carolyn wanted her daughter's room to be perfect. The upcoming weekend was all theirs. She was more excited than a six-year-old on Christmas Eve.

Her mother was trying hard to mend their broken relationship. She came by often. Carolyn never refused to let her in the house, but it was hard to let her back into her heart. The pain she had endured could have been avoided. The child was hers, and they made decisions without her. Fifteen was young, but she was still her mother.

"Carolyn!"

Hearing her mother's voice, she reluctantly walked downstairs to unlock the screen door.

"Girl, why you got this door open like this?"

"Airing out the house, Mom. The screen was locked. What brings you by?"

"Susan called and said that Vivian was coming down here for the weekend."

"She is."

"That's nice, real nice. How are you two getting along?"

"We are just fine, Momma. Is there something you need?"

"I just wanted to see you."

"Momma, I really don't want to get into it with you."

"Look, baby. I was broke, and I did what I thought was best for all concerned. You were right. I should have told you she was with your aunt. And I did not sell my grandchild. I had to pay that money back. Susan loaned me the down payment money. She sent the other money for you. I was supposed to put it up, and I didn't. I used it to keep us afloat until I got on at the plant. I love you, Carolyn, and I want you to know that. You and Vanessa were all I had. Her daddy left me for another woman, and your daddy died. I had two girls and no help."

She listened to her mother and nodded when necessary. Maybe she was sincere, but Carolyn was not ready to forgive her yet.

***

Vivian had been on an emotional roller coaster for the past few weeks. Every family had its secrets; she just didn't know that for her family she was it. She fueled her vehicle and started out. She could have easily taken a plane, but she wanted to drive her own car. Vivian carefully loaded her car. She wanted to make sure she had enough clothes. She had told Carolyn she would be there for the weekend, but actually had taken off three weeks. She wanted to know her mother and her father. She refused to come back until she met him.

Taking the long drive would give her time to think. She was happy her mother had taken her. She had the best of everything. Having older parents meant she had to deal with some things the other kids did not, but she loved them just the same. Her mom was overprotective and rarely let her hang out. She used to hate that about her, but now that she was older, she thanked God for it.

The next few weeks she planned to find out about her biological parents. She wondered if she had any siblings. Carolyn never had any more children, but her father may have. She hoped he lived in the same town. Carolyn was reluctant to divulge any information about him. If she didn't tell her, she would just have to find out on her own. She knew that Carolyn loved the man that fathered her, but that was all she knew. She had three weeks to find out as much as she could.

***

Carolyn was the happiest she had been in a very long time. Having her daughter with her all week was more than she could have hoped for. The time was going by quickly. The majority of their time was spent talking.

Vivian wanted to know as much as possible. Carolyn listened to Vivian and agreed she had a right to know her father. After two weeks of asking and pleading with her, Carolyn was still hesitating but felt compelled to at least tell her his name, so she did.

"Thank you. This means a lot to me," said Vivian.

"I know it does, just like finding you meant the world to me. There are some things you should know about your father."

"What things?"

"Well, for one, he has another daughter."

"Really? I have a sister? Do you know where she lives? Do you know where my dad lives?"

"Wait."

"What? Why won't you tell me anything?"

"Vivian, you have seen your father."

"What are you talking about?"

"Do you remember the tall man at Vanessa's funeral?"

"The one Auntie was yelling at? Of course, I do."

Carolyn looked at her daughter. Then, she placed her hand on her cheek.

"NO."

"Yes."

"I thought he was the father of Vanessa's baby, Brenda."

"He is."

"I'm confused. Why would he?"

"He didn't know that we were sisters, and she never knew about you."

Carolyn spent a few minutes explaining the details of her conception and how she was able to keep the pregnancy a secret from Vanessa who was away at college.

"I never saw him again until the day Brenda was born. I never had the nerve to tell Vanessa. She went to her grave not knowing."

"So, my father doesn't know that I exist?"

"Right now, he doesn't know."

***

Walt arrived home cheerful and full of excitement. Several days after seeing his son, he was still humming to himself. For years, he envied his brothers; each of them had sons. He wished he could have seen his son grow up, but he was happy all the same just to know he had one.

Meeting his son kept him in a jovial mood. He took his wife out dancing and to the movies. He felt like a kid again.

"What has gotten into you, Walt?" asked his wife.

"I'm just happy. I have a wonderful wife and a wonderful life," he responded as he placed a smack on her lips.

"You saw her, didn't you?"

"Saw who?"

"Claire."

"Yes, but only briefly."

"Did you sleep with her?"

"What? Of course not, Belle, those days are over. I promised you, and I meant it. I was only there to meet my son. I saw her for maybe ten minutes."

"How can I trust you?"

"You could have come with me. I did offer. Look, I know I was not faithful in the past, but I'm not that kind of man anymore. You have to believe me."

"Walt, I'm trying."

"Look, my son is getting married in a few weeks. I want to go, and I want you to come with me. We can make a weekend out of it."

"I don't know if I want to do that. There are too many bad memories."

"Belle, we have to get past this."

"I know, but it isn't easy."

"I know that, but this is my only child. I want to be a part of his life. I need you to understand that."

Belle walked away from him and took a seat on the nearby settee. She looked at him and said, "Just give me some time to think about it.

"Belle, I am going to my son's wedding. I want you to come with me. I know the affairs have been an issue with us and having a child is a big one, but together we can face this."

"It's not as easy to forget, Walt. I know that was not the only woman, but it is different. That indiscretion resulted in a child."

He pulled her into his arms and looked at her lovingly and said, "I know you can't and won't forget, but that is not what I'm asking you to do. I'm asking you to forgive me."

***

Claire sat on her sofa and started a new pattern. She loved to crochet. Even though she only worked part-time, she was often too busy to enjoy the craft. She started in on her project and was interrupted by the phone as soon as she got comfortable.

"Hello."

"Hi, Mom."

After a moment of awkward silence, she finally spoke. "So, you met him."

"Yes, ma'am."

"Son, I'm sorry it took this long for you to meet him. I was wrong and should have told you something. I was hurt and dealt with it the best way I knew how."

"He told me what happened. I'm not mad at you, Mom."

"That's good to know. So, what's new?"

"I just wanted you to know he may come to the wedding. I didn't want it to be a surprise to you if he shows."

"Thank you for letting me know."

"Mom?"

"Yes, son?"

"I just want you to know you did a great job without him, and I'm proud to be your son. I love you."

"Love you too, baby."

After her son hung up the phone, she shed the tears she didn't know she was holding on to. The life she expected to live was not what she got. She made the best of what she had, though. Sixteen was very young to have a child, but she did what needed to be done.

Tonya

Chapter 21

With the wedding only a week away, Joy wanted to make sure she had enough coverage at the hotel while she was away on her honeymoon. Her honeymoon was the only thing she was allowed to plan. Brendan's mother had agreed to keep the baby while they were away.

Tiffany was in training and doing well. She had hired a new desk clerk for second shift, and he was being trained at another property. Everything was falling into place. Once she was more comfortable with Tiffany, she planned to delegate more and take more time for herself.

Her soon to be mother-in-law had warned her about Tiffany, but so far things had been working out fine. Until she was given a reason not to, she trusted her to do her job.

Joy had booked a seven-day honeymoon cruise as a surprise. She knew Brendan had only taken off a week, and she wanted him to have time to rest before going back to work. Her mother reluctantly agreed to have the wedding locally. Joy didn't want to have to travel to get married and then get on a boat.

Since the honeymoon was the only thing she planned, she spoke with her mother almost daily to keep up with the wedding plans.

"Mom, the hotel ballroom will be just fine. I don't want a super large reception anyway. We can decorate the room after we finish at the church. I don't want a big to-do. It will be fun."

"Yeah, okay, baby," she said, sounding disappointed.

"I'll come down a few days before the wedding."

"That will be great. How are things on your end?"

"Fine, I guess."

"What's wrong, Joy?"

"I can't stop thinking about Portia. We haven't spoken in weeks."

"You told me about that."

"I'm tired of always being the bigger person, but for some reason, I think she needs me," Joy said.

"Well, what are you going to do about it?"

"I'll call her."

"Well, you do that, and let me finish up here. I'll call you if I need to."

"Okay, Mom, love you!"

Joy disconnected the call and immediately dialed Portia's cell. She redialed the number but got the same recording. Well, it had been a while. She couldn't blame her for changing the number. She decided to reach out to a mutual friend.

"Chloe, hi."

"Hey, Joy! It's been a while."

"Yeah, I know. I have been so busy."

"Yeah, I heard you were engaged."

"Yes, the wedding will be soon. I sent you an invitation."

"Good, you know that I'll be there."

"Great! Well, anyway I was wondering if you have talked to Portia lately."

"No, I haven't," Chloe said. "She changed her number apparently 'cause I tried to call her a few weeks ago."

"Hmm. Okay, well, that's all I really wanted," Joy said.

"Talk to you soon?"

"Yeah, girl, if I can get away, maybe we can do lunch."

"Sounds good, Joy."

"Bye girl."

Joy reached out to a few other friends and received similar responses. She didn't know what was going on, but she knew something wasn't right. Putting Portia out of her mind for a while, she concentrated on her work and solidifying her wedding plans. There were a few things she wanted to purchase for the cruise, and she also wanted a dress for after the wedding.

She left work early to pick up a dress that she'd ordered. The boutique was a bit crowded, so she picked out a few more items while the clerk waited on the customers in line.

"Hi, I need to pick up my order," she said to the clerk.

"Yes, ma'am. What name please?"

"Spicer, Joy," she stated

The clerk retrieved the dress and laid it on the counter. "Do you want to try it on first?"

"Yes, just in case."

"The dressing rooms are open. Let me know if you need anything else."

"Thanks." Joy walked to the back and pulled on the first dressing room door. When it didn't budge, she opened the next one. "Oh, excuse me, ma'am. I didn't know anyone was in here."

"Joy?"

"Portia?"

Joy walked in and closed the door behind her. She barely recognized Portia. Her long weave was gone. Her skin was dull, and the color was off. She also noticed old and healing bruises. Portia was always a stickler for protecting her skin. She had never seen her with a blemish.

"Oh, Portia, what happened?"

"He did it," she said in a small whisper.

"Your husband did this to you?"

"Yes."

"Why didn't you leave?"

"It's not that easy, Joy."

"Yes, it is. We can leave right now."

"I have more than me to think about now."

"What do you mean?"

"I'm pregnant."

"So! That doesn't matter, at all. You don't have to take this."

"It's better now."

"Better? How is it better? Look at yourself. Don't you see what he has done to you?"

"He hasn't touched me in a long time, and he is so happy about the baby."

"Portia, this man could kill you. Why would you stay with him?"

"I don't have anywhere to go."

"You can stay with us. You can get a job and go from there."

"Joy, I will be okay. Things have changed. Two weeks ago, I would have left with you, but now I think it is best that I stay." Portia turned and picked up Joy's dress. "This is beautiful. What is the occasion?"

"It is for after the wedding."

"Maybe I will come."

"Portia, I ..."

"Don't Joy. Just leave it alone. I will be fine."

***

Back at home, Portia let her mind go back to the conversation with Joy. She made some excellent points. Joy had barely recognized her. She stood and looked at herself in the full-length mirror in the corner of her closet. Portia barely recognized herself. Her skin was blotchy and dull. Her short hair was parted on the side and smoothed down. She looked nothing like the confident woman she was before the wedding. When did she lose herself?

Her marriage was literally draining her. How could she raise a child in this environment? How long would her husband refrain from hitting her? Should she risk staying only to find that he hadn't changed at all? She wrestled with the questions that filled her mind. After a few minutes, she decided Joy was right. It wasn't worth it. She had to find a way out.

"Portia?"

"I'm in the closet."

"Oh, I see the bags. Did you have a nice time shopping?"

"Yes, I did. I ran into my friend."

"Oh yeah?"

"Yes, her wedding is soon. I would like to go."

"Of course, so what did the doctor say today?"

"All is well. Looks like we conceived on our honeymoon."

He smiled and placed his hand on her midsection. Then, her husband walked out of the room. She watched him leave. Since finding out she was pregnant, he had been attentive and seemed genuinely concerned. She had to remind herself he was still the same man that had beaten her.

She walked over to her bed. Thanks to the plush carpet, her footsteps didn't make a sound. Portia thought about the things Joy said and realized she was right. Her husband was abusive and may never change. She had to leave. Things were not worth her life or the life of her child. She sat on her bed and began to plan her future. She went to her make-up desk and planned her escape. She realized just how blind she had been. In her pursuit of riches, she lost herself.

Portia called her mother using an app on her tablet. Her mother was surprised to hear from her since she was under the impression she was out of the country.

"What are you talking about, Mom. I've been back from my honeymoon for weeks. I lost my cell phone, and for some reason, I couldn't get through to you on the house phone."

"Well, I just got a postcard from you saying that you were overseas."

"Mom, I never sent you a postcard."

As she was uttering those words to her mother, she knew then he had planned to kill her. If her family thought she was killed out of the country, they would not look for her body here.

"Portia!"

"Mom, I'm sorry. I was calling to let you know I would be out to see you at the end of the week."

"Really? That is great! What day?"

"I'm not sure yet, but I will call before I come."

"Okay. Just let me know so I can cook all your favorites."

"Yes, ma'am. Well, Mom, I have to go. Talk to you soon."

She ended the call with her mother and worked on her escape plan. Using her app, she sent a text to secure some funds. She had to act quickly.

***

It was hard to leave Portia in the boutique, but there was nothing Joy could do or say to convince her to leave her husband. Joy took her time getting home. When she finally pulled into the driveway, Brendan was standing in the door.

"Where have you been? Why did you turn off your phone? Do you know how worried I was?" He fired questions at her faster than she could answer.

She went inside and told him about her day. She told him about seeing Portia and how much trouble she was in. "I can't believe she won't just leave."

"Joy, you can't make her leave. She is a grown woman."

"I know that, but you didn't see her. She needs help."

"So, what are you going to do, go and drag her out of there?"

"She is my friend."

"I know, and this is hard, but you can't make her leave. She has to want to go."

"I know."

"You and I have a wedding in a matter of days that needs to be your main concern. Portia will take care of Portia."

"Brendan, that sounds so selfish."

"Look, you know now, and she knows that you know and are willing to help. She will call you if she needs you."

"I hope so."

"I know you are concerned about your friend." He eased her unto his lap and said, "It will be okay." He said those words to calm her down, but he wasn't so sure himself.

***

In only a few days, he would be married. Brendan tried on his tuxedo and admired his handsome reflection in the full-sized mirrors. The man staring back at him was not the man from a year ago. This version of him was new and improved. He felt Joy was the reason for that improvement. He had always been a ladies' man, but now he had a real lady. He turned and looked at his cousin who was supposed to be trying on a tux, as well. Junior was busy trying to get the seamstress's phone number. Brendan shook his head and thanked God he wasn't looking for hook-ups anymore.

"What are you cheesing about man?" asked Junior.

"Oh, nothing really, just thinking about Joy. I didn't know I was smiling."

"Man, I'm happy to see you this happy. You know I really thought you would have married Gloria. I mean, you guys were together for a minute."

"Yeah, I know, but she wasn't what I wanted for a wife."

"And Tiffany was?"

"No not really," he answered truthfully

"Well, why did you marry her? Never mind, I get it. The baby, right?"

"Yeah."

"I understand. You were trying to do the right thing. She is cute and all, but man, that girl was too young and too wild."

"I know, but it is over now, and I have the right one finally."

Inside the fitting room, as he undressed, he thought about his first wedding. With her, he felt obligated because of her pregnancy. There was love for the child, but he was not in love with her. Tiffany was young and cute. To him, she was just an ego boost. He liked showing her off. He would have broken things off with her sooner, but her pregnancy made him change his mind.

He then thought about Gloria. As a very young man, he moved in with her. He felt guilty about how things ended, but he knew she was not what he wanted in a wife. Against his mother's wishes, he moved in with her. He told himself it would only be temporary. He was not in love but lust. She gave him an ultimatum to marry her or else, so he left. He didn't know how to tell her, but the ultimatum gave him the out he needed.

When they finally finished with the fitting, he decided to drop in and see Joy. He didn't have to hurry home. His mother and mother-in-law were there at their house spoiling the baby. Pulling up to the hotel, Brendan disposed of his cigarette and walked into the lobby. He peeped into Joy's office, but he found it empty. He journeyed over to the front desk and found Tiffany waiting on a guest. While he waited, he casually looked at his ex-wife. He noticed her very professional attire. Her uniform was immaculate, and her hair was done up in a sleek bun. This was not the Tiffany he knew.

When she was done with her customer, he walked up to the counter.

"Hi, I'm looking for Joy."

"She is in a staff meeting upstairs, but I think it's about over."

"Thanks."

"Sure, no problem."

"Slim?"

"Yeah, what's up?"

"I'm sorry for everything."

He looked at her as if she grew another head.

"What?"

"I took advantage of you. You were a good husband, and I'm happy you found someone who loves you the right way."

"Thanks, Tiffany." He realized the changes in her were more than her attire. She was maturing. He started to walk away but turned back and said, "It is good to see this side of you."

She smiled showing her cute dimples. Seeing her smile reminded him of how things were in the beginning. He would have said more, but Joy rounded the corner at that precise moment.

"Brendan?"

"Hey, I just stopped by. We got the tuxes, and so my job is done."

"Okay, great! I'll be home soon, just a few last minute things to finish."

"I'm about to run to the store to get a few more things for our houseguests. Did you want anything in particular?"

"Cookies and cream ice cream would be nice."

"Okay," he said and headed out of the door.

Joy didn't miss the guilty looks on Brendon's and Tiffany's faces and wondered what their conversation was about. She went into her office and finished up for the day. She wasn't insecure, but it didn't hurt to be careful.

Joy logged out of the computer and closed the blinds. She had decided to leave early. The wedding was in three days, and now she had cold feet. Usually, she would have called Portia or Tristan, but instead, retail therapy would have to do.

"Joy, you have a package," Tiffany said, walking into her office.

"Just put it on my desk. I'll deal with it tomorrow."

"It came from a law office."

"What? Let me see that. Thanks."

She opened the large envelope and sat down at her desk. She didn't realize she was crying until a tear dropped on the page. Morris had passed away. His lawyer had been trying to reach her. She called the number listed on the letter, and luckily, he was able to see her.

***

"When did he pass away? What happened?"

"Morris died in his sleep two weeks ago. He had cancer."

"What does all this mean?"

"He left a letter," the lawyer said, passing a thick envelope to her.

She took the envelope and put it in her purse.

"What property is the letter referring to?"

"Your hus—, excuse me, ex-husband owned several pieces of property and also a small apartment building. He left them to you along with approximately three point five million dollars in cash. You also have the responsibility of taking care of his sister, Rachel."

Joy sat speechlessly. The lawyer gave her all the info she needed, and she left the office in a daze. She sat in her car and cried until she couldn't cry anymore.

She went to the mall as planned but wandered in and out of the various shops. She stopped at the food court and ordered a cup of ice cream. She pulled the letter from her purse and placed it on the table. She stared at it as she ate her ice cream. Finally, she opened it.

If you are reading this, well, you know the rest. So, I will get to the point. I am leaving this place with only one regret, and that is you. I regret not being the husband you deserved. I am sorry. I know that I should have come clean, but I was a fool. I want you to know that I love you and I hope you find the right one. I have one final request, be happy.

In this envelope, you have all that you need to gain access to all that I have. I have willed everything to you.

Joy stopped reading and put the letter back into the envelope. She wasn't in love with him anymore, but she never wanted him dead. The rest of the evening was a blur. With her mother in the house, she literally didn't have time to grieve. She bottled up her feelings and helped her mother with the final preparations for the wedding. Brendan knew something was wrong, but when she refused to talk about it, he let it go. Joy assured him everything was alright. The next few days went by quickly. She focused on her wedding and upcoming honeymoon.

In keeping with tradition, Slim spent the night before the wedding with his best man. After a lavish rehearsal dinner with the wedding party, the cousins headed to Junior's apartment. The ladies were staying to finish some last-minute decorations for the main event.

"So, you are doing it again, huh, man?" Junior asked Slim.

"Yep, this time I know it is right. I never had a woman down for me like this before."

"Yeah, I understand that, and it don't hurt that she is fine as hell."

Slim chuckled and grabbed a bag of chips Junior had on the table and plopped down on the sofa.

"Hey, since you refuse to have a bachelor party, let's go and hit up a night spot or something. I mean, it is your last night as a free man," Junior suggested.

"The fact that you used the words 'night spot' lets me know that we are too old for that," Slim replied, shaking his head.

"Okay, okay, whatever you say. It's your day. How about we watch a movie or something?" Junior suggested, turning on the TV.

Slim relaxed on the sofa and tuned out Junior and the movie they were supposed to be watching. He felt he was finally doing it with the right one. Joy was different. He was used to women finding him attractive. For years, he used it to his advantage whenever possible. Joy was genuinely interested in him.

It wasn't until he married Tiffany that he realized how much he was missing. Family was everything to him now. Even though it didn't work out with Tiffany, it hadn't discouraged him from marriage. This time, he knew he was making the right decision.

He had another decision to make. The plant was steady work and paid well but not what he wanted to do for the rest of his life. He wanted to open up a business, maybe a small restaurant. Cooking had always been a passion of his, and with the money from his 401k and perhaps a little money from his newfound wealth, he may be able to make that a reality. He felt it was time for him to work for himself. After a while, he decided to call it a night. He wanted to be well rested for the next day. He wanted to safe all of his strength for his honeymoon.

***

Joy sat in the chair while the make-up artist worked his magic.

"Hold your head up, please."

Joy did as instructed as she relaxed on the chair. Once he finished, her newly blow-dried hair was next. The hair stylist got busy arranging her hair into an elaborate bun. Soft curls were arranged to frame her face. Joy felt like royalty with all the pampering. Her mother had gone overboard as usual. Finally finished, all she had to do was slip on her dress.

"My, my, don't you look nice."

"Portia! You made it!"

"Yes, I did," she said with a huge grin.

"You look great. I love your hair."

"Thanks and you look good enough to marry." They both laughed. "So are you ready?" Portia asked.

"More than ready! How are you doing?"

"I'm great. I'm taking your advice."

"Really! Oh, Portia, do you need anything?"

"No, I have everything that I need," she said placing her hand on her midsection."

"Where are you going?" Joy asked.

"It's better if you don't know.

"Please be careful."

"I will," Portia said, looking hopeful, which caused Joy to tear up. "Oh no, don't cry. You will mess up the make-up. Come on here, and let's get you dressed."

The two old friends walked arm and arm into the dressing room. The joy of the day was dampened a little. Joy knew, if she saw Portia again, it would be a long time.

Chapter 22

Brendan nervously stood at the altar. The entire room smelled heavily of fresh cut flowers. There was a string quartet playing soft music behind him. He tried to listen to the soloist, but he could not concentrate. Elegance is the only word he could use to describe what he saw. He glanced nervously at his best man in an attempt to calm himself. The first notes of the wedding march sounded, and his heart skipped a beat. He turned facing the aisle and watched the flower girl sauntered down the aisle.

He chuckled when he realized the little flower girl didn't drop any flowers. During the rehearsal, she pretended to throw flowers and didn't know to throw them now. Her small blunder eased his tension – a little. The pianist signaled the arrival of the bride with a few loud notes. Brendan's eyes widened at first sight of her.

Nothing could have prepared him for this moment. There she stood in a long, form-fitting champagne-colored gown. She was simply breathtaking. As his bride walked towards him, he felt the need to pinch himself. He had to be dreaming. He was minutes away from marrying the woman of his dreams. He slowly exhaled as she came towards him. As instructed, he recited his vows. When told to do so, he tenderly kissed his new wife. The wedding ceremony was over quickly. Brendan beamed with pride as he and his new bride walked slowly down the aisle for the first time as man and wife.

After the ceremony, the couple sequestered themselves in the dressing room.

"Turn around and let me help you out of that dress," he said. He slid his hands over her back and kissed the back of her neck before he undid the tiny buttons.

Joy turned and faced him as the dress slid to the floor. "Mr. McNair we have guests waiting," she reminded him.

"Let them wait," he said.

Joy smiled and helped him undress.

They were so busy consummating their marriage that they almost forgot about having to take photos. A year ago, he never would have thought he would be this happy. He'd promised her that the quickie in the dressing room was only a sample of what was to come on the honeymoon.

Brendan spent the majority of the reception looking at his brand new wife. He had to constantly remind himself it wasn't all a dream. He scanned the room and smiled at the many well-wishers in attendance. His father was there as he had hoped. One thing he didn't count on was his father bringing his wife. She was obviously uncomfortable but cordial.

He searched the sea of faces but didn't see his mother. She was not in the room, so he reluctantly left his bride to find her. Brendan found his mother outside walking towards her car.

"Mom, what are you doing out here?"

"I'm so sorry, baby. I just needed some air."

"What's wrong?"

"Her."

"Huh?"

"His wife," she stated.

"Oh."

"She lied to him and to me all these years. I can't blame her for not wanting me around her husband, but her lie denied you a father. Maybe I should have told you a long time ago. But I just buried it all."

"Mom, you did what you thought was right." "He placed his arms around her and held her. "Let's go inside."

Once inside, he danced with his mother. It wasn't long before he had her laughing.

***

Tiffany was munching on the fruit and finger sandwiches from the reception. Joy had graciously invited her employees to the reception; however, Tiffany was on duty, so she had to settle for a to-go plate. She was busy closing out reports and updating room statuses and didn't notice a man approaching the counter.

"Yes, sir, how can I help you?"

"Well, I am looking for the reception."

Tiffany admired his biceps. She let her gaze settle on his rock hard chest. This man was too fine.

"Ma'am?"

"Hmm, oh down the hall, ballroom B."

"Thanks, Tiffany"

"How did you know my name?"

"Name tag," he said pointing to the silver tag on her shirt.

"Oh yeah," she said slightly embarrassed.

He gave her a smile then walked away.

Reggie walked into the lobby a few minutes later.

"Tiffany."

"What do you need?"

"I want to see my children."

"Look, I don't have time for this. I'm on my job."

"Here," he said, laying a few large bills on the counter. "I'm working now. I can help with them now. I just want to see them. That's all I am asking for."

"We can talk about this later when I'm not at work."

"Tiffany, they are my children too."

"I know that, but this is not the time or place for this discussion. Give me a number where I can reach you."

"So, it's like that?"

"Just like that."

He gave her his number and address then walked away. She let out a breath and leaned on the counter for a few minutes. She was glad he didn't cause a scene. This job was all she had. She looked down at the money he left. She was surprised, to say the least. Extra money was always needed especially with two growing kids. She looked up in time to see the man from earlier come around the corner.

"That was fast," she said smiling showing off her dimples.

"I was just dropping off a gift," he replied.

"Oh, okay."

"Say, what time do you get off?" he asked.

She laughed at his corny line but gave him her number anyway, while inwardly thinking the drought was about to be over. He was obviously a bit older, but that never bothered her. She always felt experienced men knew how to do right.

Tristan got in his car and drove home. He couldn't make himself go to the wedding. He went to the reception, but after dropping his gift on the table, he felt it was time to leave. He saw the look on her face, and she was delighted. It was time to let it go. He thought about the attractive clerk at the desk, Tiffany. She looked to be a bit young, so he knew it wouldn't last too long. Just long enough to make him feel better.

***

Portia walked out of the church and got into the waiting car. Her husband was inside waiting, just as she expected him to be.

"How was the ceremony?" he asked without looking up from the paperwork he had on his lap.

"It was nice and elegant."

"No reception?"

"Yes, she is having one, but I don't feel like going. I need a nap."

"Yes, growing a baby is hard work," her husband said, making an attempt to be humorous. She smiled and kept up with the small talk. "Home sweet home, so are you coming?

"No, I have a bit of business to take care of."

She accepted his lame excuse and went into the house. Portia knew it would be best to travel light, so her bags included essentials only. Using her text app, she sent another message and then called a cab. Minutes later, she walked out of the house, got into the cab, and didn't look back. Arriving at the airport, she got out of the cab and waited on the driver.

"Do you mind helping me with my bag?" she asked while fanning herself with the plane tickets.

"Sure, no problem."

The driver took the fare and tip with a smile.

Portia watched the cab until it was out of sight before she walked to the desk to pick up her keys to the rental car. She knew her husband might be able to find out where the cab took her. She wanted him to think she took a flight. She had a car rental using an alias. Her destination was a few hundred miles away.

She got behind the wheel and put on her shades. Portia was a survivor. Until she felt safe, she was heading to a house out of the city. The house would not be extravagant. There wouldn't be servants or six-thousand dollar dresses hanging in the closet. Despite all that, she smiled as she thought about the fact that each mile she drove put her closer to freedom.

Chapter 23

Brendan carefully got out of bed. He didn't want to wake his sleeping bride. They had to drive out at dawn to make the plane. He was tired but too excited to sleep. He stepped out unto the balcony and watched the waves. *Never thought I would see anything like this,* he thought to himself. This was his first cruise but wouldn't be his last if he could help it. He decided to take a walk and explore the ship. He slipped on a pair of jeans and grabbed his room key.

The ship had so much to offer from shopping to theatres and even salons. He saw there was a movie playing in a few hours that he wanted to see. He walked up to the top deck and found a few people taking advantage of the pool. *This is the life*, he thought.

"Excuse me, sir, do you know the way to the … Brendan?"

Gloria stopped mid-sentence. Seeing him brought back all the anger, and she wanted to hurt him just like he hurt her. Six years of her life she could not get back was dedicated to that man. She thought for sure he would propose on her thirtieth birthday. When that didn't happen, she took her friends' advice and gave him an ultimatum. That was the last time she saw him.

"Hello, Gloria."

"Wow, I never thought I would see you again."

"Well, here I am. How have you been?" Brendan asked.

"I'm good."

"Well, it was good to see you again, but I have to go."

"So, no apology or nothing. You are just gonna leave again?" Gloria asked.

"Apologize for what? You gave me an ultimatum. I chose not to propose, and I left. It's as simple as that. Look, Gloria, I'm here to enjoy this cruise, and I don't have time for this."

"Does she know what kind of asshole you are?" she asked.

"Who?"

"I'm sure you are not on this cruise alone."

"Goodbye, Gloria."

"Brendan!"

He continued walking. He didn't know if it was just a coincidence or just bad luck. All the cruises available, she had to be on his honeymoon cruise. As he walked away, he hoped she wouldn't cause a scene. He knew she had a temper. He turned the corner and took the stairs. He carefully blended in with the crowd until he saw the stairs leading to his room. Brendan walked into his room and found Joy up and getting dressed. His mood immediately changed.

"Dinner is at eight for us. So, what do you want to do until then?" she asked.

"There is a movie I want to see tonight. We can go to the early showing and then dinner."

"Deal," she said, planting a kiss on his lips.

Throwing Gloria out of his mind, Brendan took his bride by the hand and led the way. Over dinner, he told Joy about his relationship with Gloria and her being on the boat. Joy told him about the will and money left to her. When she told him how much, Brendan nearly choked on his appetizer.

"What?" he asked gasping for air.

"Close to four million," she said.

"Dollars?"

"Yes, Brendan."

"Wow!"

"There are some other things too."

"Like what?"

"We now own an apartment building. When we get home, I will sort everything out and see what we need to do. I don't know what kind of condition it's in. I don't know if I have to make improvements. Also, he asks that I be responsible for his sister if need be."

"His sister?"

"Yes, Rachel."

"Why do you have to take care of her? Is she sick or something?"

"No, she is very young. She is actually his half-sister. His father had an affair several years ago, and she is the result."

"How old is she?"

"She should be about sixteen or seventeen by now. Her mother was in and out of rehab. Morris used to make sure she had what she needed. She was all the family he had left after his parents died. I haven't seen her since he and I divorced."

"Wow."

"When we get back, I will try to contact her. I'm just trying to figure out how I will be able to fit this in with work and all."

"Joy, we don't have to work. We can retire and live off the revenue from the properties."

"True, that is an option. But let's talk about it after we get home. I just want to have my honeymoon."

"Whatever you say, pretty lady." He smiled to himself, thinking, *I am going to quit my job on Monday.*

Gloria chose that moment to walk over to their table. "Brendan, why don't you introduce me to your friend?"

"Wife," Joy said, not taking the bait.

"Wife?" Gloria asked in a hoarse whisper.

"Yes, as in Mrs. McNair," Joy replied while holding up her left hand.

Brendan didn't say a word.

"Did you need something?" Joy asked.

Defeated, Gloria turned and left.

That night, he could barely sleep. Brendan sat on the balcony while his wife slept. He let out a breath and sighed with relief. He had hoped he wouldn't see Gloria again but knew that was very unlikely. Thankfully, he had already told his wife about her.

Millions. He could barely wrap his mind around it. That was a lot of money. Joy seemed to have a better handle on this situation than he did. All he could think was his luck was changing. They had agreed not to talk about the money, so he spent the rest of the cruise finding ways to make his wife scream. He kissed, licked, and tasted every part of her.

On the last day of the cruise, disembark was at 10 a.m. They tagged their bags and walked to the airport shuttle. The short flight home landed on time. Brendan loaded the car then slid behind the wheel. He smiled at his new bride and found a song on the radio.

They arrived home to find a strange car in the driveway.

"Baby, whose car is that?" he asked.

"I was about to ask you," she replied. "Maybe your mom has company."

"That could be it. I'll just park behind Mom's car. Go on in. I'll get the bags."

"Okay."

Brendan walked in, dropped the luggage in their bedroom, and headed to the kitchen. He was shocked to see Carolyn coming out of the hall bathroom.

"Carolyn? What's going on? What are you doing here?"

"I need to talk to you."

"Why didn't you just call me? Is something wrong?"

"There is someone I need you to meet."

"What? Who is it?"

"Please come with me."

Reluctantly, he followed her out to the patio. Joy sat next to his mother and across from her was the young lady he saw at the funeral.

"Carolyn, what's going on?"

She walked over to stand next to the young lady and said, "Brendan this is Vivian. She is your daughter. She is our daughter."

To be continued…

CPSIA information can be obtained
at www.ICGtesting.com
Printed in the USA
LVHW031749211119
638114LV00014B/994/P